The Disappearance of Tommy Hill

By, A. A. Smith

Written by

A.A. Smith

Chapter 1

Sherry had just finished with her last patient when the call came in. A young girl arriving was having seizures. She had been a nurse at the hospital for the last two years. Her shift was ending in 30 minutes and she breathed a sigh of relief, realizing the girl hadn't arrived yet and hoping she wouldn't be forced to work overtime. She quickly grabbed the phone and called up to request a room in the emergency department.

She noted the flashing lights pulling in through the windows. She was rushed in with an IV already attached.

"She is still convulsing." The paramedic said, "We have given Diazepam and she is showing no signs of stopping."

"Do you know any history on her?" Sherry asked.

"No."

"Do we know her name yet? Any family contacts?"

"No." He replied as they rushed her to a room

Froth and blood were pooling from her mouth.

"She must have bitten her tongue." Sherry thought out loud.

The girl's head was thrown back with muscles tense and jerking. She didn't have any identification on her and they were unable to determine if she had seized before. She appeared to be near twenty. She was thin and frail with long blonde hair. She was still seizing when the doctor on duty arrived. The paramedics reported that she seized since they had been dispatched to pick her up at the theatre. They reported that no one knew her at the scene. The doctor quickly ordered dose of Lorazepam. Sherry quickly gave it through her IV and they waited several minutes as she continued to convulse. The doctor ordered another dose, she administered it. They waited again.

Her convulsions slowed, then she went limp. She was still breathing but unconscious. Her blood pressure was very low. Her heart rate was slow.

"Let's monitor her for several hours for any activity. If she awakens, notify me ASAP." The doctor said.

Sherry turned to check the monitors as the paramedics exited her room. Her heart rate was 54 but steady. She insured her IV was safe before exiting.

Sherry glanced back at the patient. The young girl appeared to be in a deep sleep. She situated the call light on the bed rail. She turned to insure the monitors were all working. Suddenly, she felt someone grab her arm. She turned to note that the girl had sat up. Her eyes were open but appeared glazed and in a trance. She tilted her head towards her.

"Why did they hurt me? Tommy was a good boy. Tommy loved everybody. Why was he so mean to Tommy?" The patient said.

Sherry's heart was racing. The girl was squeezing her arm. She had the strength of a man. She watched wide eyed, unable to catch her breath. She appeared as a child and yet her voice was that of a grown man, deep and strong. She fell back with her head on the pillow and was unconscious again. She appeared to have never moved.

Sherry didn't speak a word about this to anyone that night. She was so shaken that she quickly reported to her relief and left. She felt as if she might have imagined the entire incident. She didn't want anyone to think that she had gone mad. Her husband was at work when she arrived home. He was working third shift and was a police officer. They had only been married for two years. He would surely think she had gone mad. She decided to dismiss the incident to being tired.

Her husband was next to her when she awoke the next morning. She still felt a little shaken by the incident but didn't speak of it. She decided a hot shower could possible help to clear her mind. She stepped off the side of the bed when her husband Joe looked at her.

"Leaving so soon beautiful?" He asked.

She turned to see his beautiful face smiling at her. She had to smile back. She jumped back into the bed and snuggled up next to him.

"I've been thinking about taking off a few days next month. I thought we could use a short vacation. What do you think? We could go up to the mountains and camp for a few days. It would be nice to breathe some fresh air and leave this city for a few days." He suggested.

"I think that would be wonderful. I will ask for the days off as soon as you tell me when."

Her husband was every girls dream. She had met him just days after moving to Phoenix. He was a native to the city. They had met at the laundromat next to her small apartment complex. They quickly connected and were married within six months. She likes to boast that it was love at first sight. Her name was Sherry Knight and nothing excites her more than changing it to Mrs. Joshua Masters. He was 10 years her elder. He had been a police officer for eight years in Phoenix and was passionate about his work. She was 27 and had moved to Phoenix for a job at the hospital after finishing nursing school in Tucson.

They had many of the same interests and connected right away. They bought a small house near the hospital and were planning a family once their finances were more secure. Lately, their weekends together had become fewer since he had friends that he went on hunting expeditions with more often than she liked but she had made friends to spend time with.

The next morning she awoke, glanced at the time and realized that she had slept later than she had planned. She quickly jumped out of bed and began fumbling around the room looking for something to wear.

"What did you do to your arm?" Joe asked.

She stopped and gave a confused look then raised her right arm to note a dark bruise near the wrist. She quickly shook her head.

"Oh, I banged it on a bed rail last night." She replied.

He walked toward her and grabbed her arm above the wrist. He gently raised it then kissed the bruise. He said, "You must have banged it hard."

"It feels better now." She smiled.

She knew now that she hadn't imagined the incident. She was anxious to find out if there were any new information on this mysterious woman. Who was she? They spent a nice morning together and she tried not to think about what had happened. They searched different camp sites and amenities then finally decided on one seventy miles away. Joe was making the plans as she readied herself for work. She kissed him goodbye and was out the door with an hour to spare.

She arrived at work anxious to inquire of the girl's condition. Miss Rose, the elderly nurse on duty was skeptical of everyone and reluctant to share information. She was a short round woman near retirement. She had gray curly hair and glasses. She reminded her of a strict school teacher.

"Good afternoon Miss Rose. How was your day?" Sherry greeted her.

"It was the same as yesterday. Thank you." Rose nodded and replied.

Sherry knew what she meant because that was always her reply. It meant busy and hectic.

"There was a young girl brought in last night near the end of my shift. I was curious how she is doing?" Sherry asked.

"I have no idea which girl you are talking about." Rose looked confused.

"She didn't have any identification. She was convulsing."

"I have no idea who you are talking about. Perhaps you should get clocked in and go to work." Rose raised her eyebrow.

"Yes, Miss Rose. "

      She had worked most of her shift without a moment's break before she was able to search the records in the computer. She didn't know how to search for her so she checked for Jane Doe. Two were showing as admitted. One was a woman approximately 50 and the other approximately 20. She knew right away which one her patient was. The records showed she was still unconscious and had been transferred to the fourth floor. She waited until her lunch break then made my way to the fourth floor.

Once she arrived at the fourth floor, the nurse at the desk seemed friendly.

"I am here to see the Jane Doe." Sherry said.

"Do you know who she might be?" The nurse asked.

"No. I was on duty last night when she came in through the emergency department. I was just curious how she is."

"She has not shown any improvement since her arrival. She is in room 432 if you want to see her."

"Thank you." Sherry slowly walked toward the room. She was telling herself in her head to just turn around and go back down stairs.

She arrived at the room with the door open. She peeked inside to see her lying with her eyes closed and still hooked up to the monitors. She slowly proceeded into the room, stepping to the end of her bed.

"Who are you?" Sherry asked as she stared at the girl. She looked innocent and small. She studied her wondering where she came from. Her nails were short and dirty. Her face was thin and pale. Her arms were skinny and appeared weak.

She appeared to be peacefully sleeping. She walked toward the drapes and began opening them, suddenly, from behind her the girl said, "Please don't tell on me. I'm sorry I didn't mean to scare you. Tommy don't like trouble. Tommy hates to get in trouble."

The same deep voice of a man but the words of a child. She quickly turned to note that she was sitting up, staring at her with the same glazed eyes in a trance. She proceeded toward her, although her heart was pounding. As she approached the foot of the bed, she seemed to go limp and fall back. A nurse walked into the room.

"Who are you? Is everything okay? We noted an increase in her heart rate on the monitors." The nurse said.

"She has been the same since I arrived." Sherry answered.

She was nervous and confused and spent the rest of her shift pondering if she should tell someone of her experience. She thought that no one would believe her and they would probably request a mental evaluation if she were to say something. The only person she could trust was Josh but he might think she was crazy also. She decided to take a wait and see approach. She finished her shift and went home and she tried to pretend everything was normal.

The next morning, Joe asked, "Is everything alright?"

"I am feeling a little under the weather but I am sure it will pass." Sherry smiled.

She was off the next day and decided to take a break. She was trying not to think about the girl. Joe left early for work and she grabbed her laptop. She did a quick search for any reports of a missing girl. Within minutes, she came across a post of a girl in Phoenix that had been missing for a week. She fit the description.

The post read:

19 year old Jane Smith missing. She was last seen in the Phoenix area and reported to have left with a boyfriend. She has a tattoo on her right thigh. The tattoo is a picture of a snake eating a rat.

She didn't want to reply to the Facebook post right away, it could prove disappointing if she were wrong. Although, the photograph bore a strong resemblance.

The woman posting the photo seemed anxious for any replies. She asked that the post be shared in hopes of finding her. She wanted to click right away and send her a message, but felt that she should wait and confirm the tattoo. She decided to pay another quick visit and verify the tattoo. She took the short drive and arrived at room 432 within minutes. Jane Doe was still unconscious and the nurse reported no changes.

Sherry entered the room quietly and proceeded to the foot of the bed.

"I don't know if you can hear me." She paused then said, "I believe your mother is searching for you. I saw a post on Facebook reporting you missing. I would like to verify that you have a tattoo on your thigh."

The girl showed no response. She walked to the side of the bed and reached down to pull the covers up near her thigh. Suddenly, Jane Doe grabbed her hand.

"What are you doing?" Jane Doe said. Her voice was young and feminine. She spoke clearly and softly.

Sherry stopped to look at her. She had opened her eyes narrowly. Sherry smiled and said, "You are awake. That is wonderful! Welcome back."

"Where am I?" Jane Doe said as she turned her head toward the window.

The nurse on duty busted through the door and said, "Is everything okay? We noted a change in the heart rate."

"She is awake. She is awake." Sherry nodded.

The nurse asked Sherry to step out for a minute. After several minutes in the hallway, she was welcomed back in.

Sherry stepped back into the room. The young girl appeared tired and weak. "I know you don't know who I am. I am a nurse that was working the night that you were brought in." She explained.

"What happened?" Jane Doe asked.

"I was hoping you could tell me."

"I don't remember anything. I don't even remember my name." The girl nodded her head.

Sherry was lost as to what to say. The girl began to cry. Sherry sat down on the side of her bed and put her hand on her shoulder.

"It will come back to you. It might take a little time, but I am sure it will all come back."

"I wish I believed that."

"Do you mind if we look and see if you have a tattoo on your thigh?" Sherry asked.

She quietly pulled her covers back. It was there, the tattoo of the snake eating the rat.

"That is great! Your mother is looking for you. Maybe seeing her will bring all of your memories back."

"Do you think so?" The girl asked with wide eyes.

"I hope so." Sherry quickly grabbed her phone and pulled up Facebook. She began searching for the post and found it right away. She sent a quick message asking her to call and within minutes her phone was ringing. She stepped outside the door to answer the call.

"I have wonderful news. I have found your daughter!" Sherry said with excitement.

"My daughter? The woman missing is not my daughter. She is a patient at the Mesa Mental institution. She escaped over a week ago." The woman paused and then said, "She ran off with a young man that worked here at the facility. She was going to be released into a rehabilitation clinic within a week. We were searching because we wanted to ensure her safety."

"This woman came in alone. Please come down and identify her. I would love to speak with you when you arrive. I work here at the hospital. I was here when she came in."

"I will be there within an hour."

Sherry walked back into the room. She was staring out the window as if she wanted to escape again.

"I'm sorry." Sherry said as she turned her head toward the young girl.

"For what?" Jane Doe looked puzzled.

"I was wrong. That was not your mother searching for you. It seems that you were in a rehabilitation clinic and left." She explained.

"A rehabilitation clinic for what?"

"Amnesia." She nodded. "Listen. We are going to figure all of this out. It might take a little while. I am sure that we can though."

"Okay." Sherry could tell she didn't really believe her.

They waited for the woman to arrive. She arrived in less than an hour. She walked in wearing a long tight skirt that went nearly to her feet that donned a pair of three inch black heels. Her hair was up in a tight bun and her make-up was flawless. She appeared to be in her fifties and struggling with her mid-life crisis. She seemed hurried from the moment she arrived.

"Jane, you should have known that men cannot be trusted. Now look at you." The woman said, but Jane Doe didn't respond. She turned her head to glare out the window.

"Please. I want to ask you something?" Sherry said.

"What?"

"If she came in with amnesia to your facility, then how did you know her name?" She asked.

"Dear, we didn't know her name. We gave her that name since she didn't have one."

Sherry nodded. The woman seemed rude and strict.

"Has she ever had seizures since being in your facility?" Sherry asked.

"Seizures? No she hasn't. Why are you asking?"

"She came in having seizures the night we admitted her."

"She probably did some drugs with David."

"David?"

"The young man that she left with." The woman said and then she looked to Jane, "Jane, you should consider yourself lucky that I even came after you. Doing something stupid like this, I should leave you here."

Jane looked down but didn't reply.

"Listen ma'am, we have a wonderful rehab unit here. Perhaps we can check into getting her admitted to ours."

Jane widened her pleading eyes at her.

"Perhaps we could. God knows I am tired of trying to help her." The woman said.

Sherry directed her to the rehabilitation wing. Sherry made sure the woman was not in earshot of them anymore and had some questions for Jane after their little reunion.

"Jane, do you remember being at her facility?" Sherry asked.

"No." Jane gazed at her with innocent eyes.

"Do you remember her at all? Does she even look familiar to you?"

"No."

Sherry wanted to help her but I didn't know how. They waited for the lady to return and within an hour, they could hear her clicking heels on the tile proceeding down the hallway.

"Jane, they are going to visit you soon here in your room. They have some nice programs that you could benefit from." The woman said before leaving the hospital.

"Jane, would you like to get out of bed and take a walk?"

She nodded.

Sherry proceeded down the hallway to the nurse's desk and asked, "Is it possible we could get a wheelchair? I believe our patient would like to get up for a bit. I'm not sure how stable she is on her feet."

"I will check with the doctor and let you know soon." The nurse at the desk said. Within a few minutes a nice nurse arrived pushing an empty wheelchair. She said,

"Please bring her back within an hour for her medicine." The nurse said.

Jane didn't have any clothes or shoes of her own. Instead, they used one hospital gown frontwards and backwards. Sherry lowered the rail as she pushed the covers off. She scooted and turned herself to edge her legs off the bed. She noted Jane's right foot was turned completely inwards. She stopped her to touch her foot.

"Can you move this foot?"

Jane looked confused as she tried to flex her foot. It appeared she could move it but not straighten her leg.

Jane was thin and petite giving the appearance of a starving child. She weighed no more than 80 pounds and her skin was pale, almost transparent. Her hair was thin and blonde and dark circles circling her eyes seemed to highlight the ocean blue color. She seemed weak and fragile as a china doll that could crack if not handled delicately.

She was unable to stand even on the left foot. Sherry carefully assisted her to the wheelchair. She folded her blanket on her bed and placed it in her lap. Jane was a woman of few words, but seemed to enjoy the walk. She watched the people moving about the hallways as if it she were in amazement. Her eyes were wide as she turned her head and looked about. Sherry took her back to her room within an hour and assisted her back to the bed. Jane still hadn't spoken a word. Sherry was preparing to leave when Jane looked up at her from the bed.

"Sherry, are you coming back?"

Sherry turned to study her face. She had a sincerity in her eyes that reminded me of a scared child.

"Of course." Sherry smiled.

"I mean you don't have to. I wouldn't blame you if you didn't." Jane said as was fighting back tears. She looked to the window then said, "It's just, you're the only person I know."

Sherry left fighting back her own tears she couldn't imagine being in her situation. She decided that she would confide to Joe about her, but she would leave the part out about a man like voice speaking to her.

She hardly slept as she listened for him to arrive home. She heard his key in the lock and quickly got out of bed sprinting to greet him. She grabbed him right away, kissing him.

"Wow. What did I do to deserve this pleasure?" Joe said, smiling.

She smiled back and said, "There is something I need to discuss with you."

"Alright." He said as he sat in a chair by the table.

"The other night, a woman was brought in by EMS seizing uncontrollably. She is stable now in a room but she has amnesia. She has nothing. No clothes, shoes, family or friends. I would like to help her."

"Okay. You don't need my permission to help someone." He said.

"I know but I wanted to tell you about it."

"That is what I love about you. You always try to help anyone that needs it. You help her however you want." He smiled.

"You are the best husband ever."

She went to sleep shortly after their conversation. She was anxious to get up early and go shopping. She wanted to buy her some clothes and perhaps a robe. She wasn't sure on her shoe size so that would have to wait. After some quick shopping, she stopped by Jane's room before her shift started. Jane seemed pleasantly surprised to see her as she entered the room smiling.

"How do you feel today?" Sherry asked.

"I feel better than yesterday. I am so glad you came by." Jane smiled.

"I have a small surprise for you." She handed her the bag with two sweat suits and a robe.

"Thank you. I really appreciate this. But, I didn't expect anything like this from you."

"I know but I wanted to."

"The doctors told me today that I am going to be transferred to the rehabilitation unit tomorrow. They seem to think that as long as I take my medicine, the seizures will be controlled." Jane said.

"That is wonderful."

Jane smiled with a frightened look on her face. Sherry sat down beside her and touched her hand.

"Listen to me. This is a process but you will get through it. If you happen to regain any memories at all, please tell me." Sherry said.

"I am trying." Jane replied.

"I know you are, but I am going to help you get through this. You're not alone."

"Thank you."

Sherry promised to return again after her shift was over. She felt as if she was obligated to help her.

After work, she hurried to Jane's room. Jane was sleeping when she arrived. She walked into her room and wasn't sure if she should wake her or let her sleep. She stood quietly at the foot of the bed, staring at her. Suddenly, Jane sat up with her eyes closed. She opened her eyes, her glazed tranced eyes.

"Why does everybody think Tommy is bad? Tommy doesn't mean to be bad." Jane began to cry in her man like voice. Then, she started to sing, "Tommy, Tommy was a big old boy. He needed a bra he could not afford. So all day long, we laughed along and sang this little song. Tommy, Tommy was a big old boy." She suddenly fell limp with her eyes closed.

Sherry's heart was pounding and her mind was racing. She wasn't sure what to do. She fled the room, feeling like a coward. She frantically drove home, still in disbelief. She arrived knowing that Joe wouldn't be home for several hours and kept telling herself to get a grip. She felt bad because she had promised Jane a visit at the end of her shift. A large part of her was telling her to never go back. The compassionate side of her however, knew that she had to. She showered and went to bed.

The next morning Josh asked, "Did you go shopping and buy some things for the young girl?"

"Yes, she was very appreciative." Sherry replied.

"Perhaps this weekend I could go with you to meet her?"

"That would be wonderful." Sherry smiled.

"I would love to meet her. Anyone that is a friend of yours is a friend of mine." Joe said and gave her a kiss.

"I feel like this is going to be a long process, but I think she is worth it."

"I am sure she is." Joe said, not knowing the extent of the situation.

Sherry felt guilty for running away last night and wondered if Jane would resent her for it. She arrived before work and was surprised to see the room had been vacated and cleaned. She quickly went to the desk.

"Jane Doe in room 432? Where is she?" Sherry asked.

The nurse smiled and replied, "She was discharged and sent to the rehabilitation unit this morning."

"Do you know which room she was placed in?"

"No. I can find out if you don't mind waiting a few minutes." The nurse replied.

Sherry nodded and smiled. She waited as she made calls inquiring.

"She was put in room 666 on the sixth floor." The nurse proclaimed.

Sherry thanked her. She decided that due to time being short, she should wait until after her shift to visit.

Her shift seemed to drag as she was anxious to see Jane. After her shift, she rushed to room 666, feeling as if Jane would be excited to her. She arrived to find Jane awake and watching television.

Sherry said smiling, "Hey, how are you doing?"

"I'm fine, thanks." Jane nonchalantly replied.

Sherry sat down beside her and said, "I am so sorry about last night. I wasn't feeling well and went straight home."

"That is fine. I totally understand." Jane gave a sarcastic smile.

"No. I don't think you do. I think you feel like I didn't want to visit and that is not true."

"No. It's fine. I wouldn't want to invest my time into someone like me either."

"You are not me. I can invest my time however I choose."

"I'm sorry. I have no right to be angry at someone that has tried to help me." Jane smiled.

"It's okay. You are afraid and I would be too." Sherry said and changed the topic of conversation. "What size shoe do you wear?"

"I have no idea." Jane smiled.

"I was afraid of that." Sherry quickly pulled out her small tape measure.

"Now that is called using your head." Jane laughed. They measured her feet and determined her shoe size is a seven.

She left anxious again to see her tomorrow and she wanted to ask her about Tommy, but felt as if the time was not right. She felt drawn to her, but couldn't understand why and wondered why she felt special to her. She was off the next day and decided she would spend it with her. She went to the local department store and bought her some personal hygiene items, undies and a pair of shoes.   When Sherry arrived to the room, Jane was sitting in her wheelchair when watching television. She slowly opened the door, making sure she was interrupting anything.

"How are you today?" Sherry greeted her.

"The therapist seems to think I will be able to walk if we work hard enough." Jane seemed excited.

"That is wonderful."

Jane was smiling and seemed overjoyed. Sherry sat down by her in the chair.

"I need to ask you a question and I want you to be honest." Sherry said.

"Of course." Jane nodded.

"Does the name Tommy mean anything to you at all?"

"No. I don't believe I have ever heard that name before. Not that I would remember anyway. Why do you ask?" Jane seemed perplexed.

Sherry quickly dismissed it and said, "Oh, never mind. I was just wondering."

"No. There is a reason that you asked me. Is there someone named Tommy that might know me?"

"I am sure it was a mistake. Please, forget I asked." Sherry quickly changed the subject and said, "My husband, Joe wants to meet you."

"You have a husband?" Jane asked.

"Yes. He is wonderful. The best thing that ever happened to me."

"That is great, maybe someday I can say that too."

Sherry laughed and said, "I am sure you will." They spent the afternoon talking. Jane asked many questions about how Joe. She seemed interested in learning about him and Sherry felt as if they were connecting on a personal level.

That evening, Sherry was excited to tell Joe about the progress that Jane was making. When he arrived home, she greeted him at the door and kissed him immediately.

"Can I go back out and do this all over again?" Joe laughed.

"Jane's rehabilitation is going well and I am so happy for her." Sherry smiled.

"That is wonderful. She might be able to get a job and get her own place soon."

"I don't know about that."

"Why?" Joe asked.

"She seems to be a little developmentally disabled. She possibly has the mind of a 10 year old, but she is adorable and I love her."

"So, she is a retard?"

Sherry stepped back in shock as the rage overtook her. She was shocked that he would say something so distasteful.

"Why would you say something like that?"

"Oh, I am sorry I shouldn't have said that."

Sherry was boiling with anger as she stormed out of the room.

Joe begged her to forgive him and promised he would never say anything like that again. Although, Sherry was still upset by his words that cut like a knife, she reluctantly forgave him. He begged her to keep him updated on Jane's progress and seemed eager when she came home telling of her progress. He seemed excited to know she was beginning to show progress. He also seemed excited to meet her the upcoming weekend.

On Friday, he came home and sadly had to cancel. He said that one of the other officers had taken an emergency leave and he would have to work. Sherry was disappointed, but understood. They decided that the next weekend they were both free would be sufficient. Sherry visited her everyday both before and after work.

In a matter of days, Jane was walking with a brace on her right foot, although, slow and with a cane. Sherry wondered if it were a birth defect or trauma that had caused her foot to turn. Social services had seen fit to help her apply for a disability check. Through some investigative work, they had determined her identification to be made legally Jane Smith.

Apparently, the place she had escaped from had filed the proper papers to make it her legal name. Sherry arrived one evening after work to find Jane leaned over in her chair. Not realizing she was asleep she strolled in announcing her arrival.

"Hey Jane. How was therapy today?" Sherry asked.

Jane raised her head with glazed blue eyes in a trance state and said, "Why wouldn't you care about Tommy? No one ever cares about Tommy. Poor, Poor Tommy Hill." In a man's voice and child words she sang, "Tommy, Tommy always sucking his thumb. Tommy, Tommy is a retarded bum."

Sherry stopped in my tracks as she sang.

"Who are you?" Sherry asked in disbelief.

"I am Tommy Hill, Will you help me, please?" Crying in her man voice she said, "Will you?" Her head fell limp.

Sherry stayed and watched over her. Shortly after, Jane seemed to be waking up. She raised her head and looked at Sherry with her beautiful blue eyes and said, "Sherry, I was afraid you wouldn't make it tonight."

Sherry smiled consolingly and said, "Of course I would make it. Let's go down to the cafeteria and grab a snack."

That night, when Sherry arrived home she quickly grabbed her laptop and googled "Tommy Hill, Phoenix Arizona." The results were many, but one in particular caught her eye.

It read:

"16 year old Tommy Hill missing since March 20, 1998. He is handicapped and feared in danger. He has the mindset of a 10 year old and his family is very concerned for his safety. Anyone with information is asked to call Mary Hill at 602-444-5666"

She wanted to call, but wasn't sure that the number was even still active. She decided to wait until morning after contemplating for several minutes. Joe arrived home as expected. Sherry elected to continue with my secret and quickly closed her laptop. She felt as if he would fear for her safety or believe that she had gone completely mad. She wasn't ready to share this information with anyone and a small part of me wondered if I hadn't gone mad.

The next morning, she awoke earlier than usual. She had tossed and turned most of the night wondering if she should or shouldn't call the number. She knew Joe would sleep at least until noon and it was only 9 in the morning. She grabbed her phone and took it with her out onto the patio. She nervously dialed the numbers. It rang several times before an elderly woman answered, "Hello."

"Yes, Could I speak to Mary Hill please?" Sherry asked.

The voice said, "This is Mary Hill can I help you?"

"I am calling about Tommy Hill." There was a silence that was deafening on the other line.

"Have you found him?" Mary asked.

"No. I haven't found him. I am sorry, but I would like to talk to you about him. I am doing some research on old cold cases and would love to gather some information."

"I already told the police everything I knew. They didn't care then so why do you care now?"

"Ma'am, with new technology available it could prove helpful in your search."

"Okay, But you will have to come to me, I don't drive anymore." Mary said.

"Yes ma'am that is fine. Can I have your address please?"

"1666 North Piney Holler. It's pretty easy to find. We live near the mountain side." Mary replied.

"Can I come this weekend? Maybe Saturday morning?"

"That is fine. I am home most of the time."

Saturday came and Joe had scheduled a hunting excursion with his friends but she was off work. It was perfect timing for her to visit Mrs. Hill. She was both nervous and anxious about the visit. She used google maps and noted it to be only an hour drive from her house. She left early that morning following the maps.   She arrived to find an old dilapidated house hidden by large trees. The paint was worn off the siding, the roof appeared to be in bad need of repair. There were several old broken down cars in the front yard. The garage doors were ripped off exposing more broken cars. The driveway was made of dirt with holes and mud. She decided to park on the street and walk to the door. It appeared there were no neighbors and this was the only house as far as she could see. She was questioning her decision to come when the door suddenly opened and a small old woman in a house dress motioned to her. Sherry smiled and got out of the car. The old woman walked very slow with a walker and proceeded toward her from the broken porch. Her right leg appeared to be turned inward as she limped forward, having to lift her left foot over her right with each step.

"I am coming please wait there." Sherry called out.

        Once Sherry reached her, she noted the woman's teeth were missing and she had chewing tobacco dripping from the corner of her mouth. Her house dress had pins holding the pockets in place on each side. Her shoes were worn and tattered exposing her big toe on the left. She quickly invited sherry into a room that was very dark with only a small lamp that was missing its shade. Her small dog came from under the table barking repeatedly.

"Yo-Yo get outta here, now get," Mary said, shewing him away.

Sherry noted the kitchen cabinets doors were missing right away. The exposed shelves were full of mason jars that donned her canning expertise of fresh vegetables.

"I am sorry. I know that it is very painful for you to have to rehash this painful time." Sherry said.

Mary sat down slowly in a rocking chair and gestured for Sherry to sit beside her on the couch that was covered with an old blanket.

"I don't know what it is you are looking for, but I reckon I owe it to Tommy to help anyway I can." Mary said.

"About Tommy? Can you tell me everything about Tommy? I mean from the time he was born to the time he disappeared?" Sherry asked.

"I reckon I don't know where to start but I can give it a try." She leaned back in her chair and said, "Tommy was my second born. We knew right away that the boy wasn't right but I loved him anyway. You know, he didn't learn fast, never did grow up as a matter of fact. His daddy was a good man, but didn't have any patience with that kind of stuff." She spit in the can next to her. She rocked slowly as she went on, "Tommy never did even learn to tie his shoes. His brother was born a few years earlier, smart as a wit. They were thick as thieves the two of them."

"Jake, was that his brother? Where is he now?" Sherry asked.

"Jake had a problem following rules. He's doing time down in Tucson now for murder. He is sitting on death row. Jake was a problem but not my Tommy. Tommy was a good boy. The only reason Tommy ever got in trouble was cause of Jake."

"What happened when he disappeared?"

"Jake always kept Tommy at his side. Jake was troubled, but he always took care of his brother. You should have seen how he was if someone made fun of Tommy. That boy would get madder than a wet hen. Jake got sent to prison and Tommy didn't know how to deal with his brother being gone. He said

27

he was going to town one day and took off walking." She wiped a tear as she said, "The boy never came back."

"I am sorry. I know that this is very difficult for you. How long has Jake been in prison?" Sherry asked.

"He got locked up just weeks before Tommy disappeared."

"Did you know of anyone that might have wanted to hurt Tommy?"

"You know the boy was special so just about everybody picked at him. The boy wasn't right! He didn't hurt nobody, though. Nobody had any reason to hurt him."

"One more question then I promise I will leave."

Mary nodded.

"Tommy, was his right foot turned in the same as yours?" Sherry asked.

"What difference would that make?" Mary seemed confused.

"It doesn't make a difference. I thought it would make him more identifiable."

Mary seemed aggravated as she looked off.

"That was a family trait I reckon. My Father had it, as did Tommy. Jake didn't inherit that trait, but then again Jake is smart. I guess I didn't do something right in raising my boys. Both of them taken away in the blink of an eye. Their daddy died a few years back and never was much count anyway." She leaned in toward Sherry and said, "You reckon my boy is still out there somewhere?"

Sherry felt guilty now for coming. She gave a consoling smile and said, "I have no idea if he is."

She wanted to give her the answer she wanted to hear but she knew better, she stood up and said, "Thank you for agreeing to see me. You have been a great help with the information you provided."

"I told you the same thing I told the police years ago." Mary laughed.

Sherry smiled and proceeded toward the door. Mary quickly proceeded toward the door behind her pushing her walker.

"I sure hope you're smarter than the police we had back then. That detective Lipton sure didn't seem the least bit interested in finding out what happened to my boy. He said, 'People like Tommy are better off disappearing. They aren't nothing but a nuisance to society anyway.'" She said, shaking her head.

Sherry turned toward her and said, "Lipton?"

"Yes, Carl Lipton I believe was his name. He was a real asshole. Never did even look for Tommy."

Chapter 2

Once Sherry arrived home, she quickly grabbed her laptop and searched the internet for Carl Lipton. The results came up right away stating that he had retired with outstanding credit in 2013. It stated that he was an outstanding officer that was always willing to help anyone. Joe arrived as she was researching Mr. Lipton.

"Why are you googling Carl Lipton?" Joe asked.

She embarrassingly said, "I had a patient come in today that was complaining about something that happened a long time ago. He said that Mr. Lipton wasn't eager to help his situation."

"I personally know Carl Lipton. I worked with him for a while. He is a very good man and an excellent police detective." Joe said.

She smiled as she closed the laptop and said, "I figured as much. You know how people can be." She reached out and threw her arms around his neck, kissing him.

After dinner, they went into the bedroom and made love, it was wonderful as always. They were lying in bed snuggling when Josh said, "Be careful listening to people's stories in this town. We have now and have always had an excellent police force."

"I'm sorry, I wasn't doubting the integrity of the police force."

"No, I'm sorry. I guess I'm just defensive when it comes to the Phoenix police force."

She rolled over to go to sleep wondering why he was so defensive.

The next day, she awoke early and had to go back to work at noon. She decided to pay a quick visit to Jane before going to work. She arrived to find Jane with her therapist walking. Jane smiled eagerly when she seen her.

"See Sherry, no hands!" Jane called out. She was gleaming as she let go of the walker to take a few steps. Sherry quickly ran to her to grab her in case she were to fall.

It had only been a month since she had been brought in and she had progressed very quickly. The therapist approached Sherry.

"Mrs. Masters, I would like to speak with you when you have a few moments to spare." The therapist said.

"I can come early tomorrow if that would be okay?"

"That would be wonderful."

Sherry arrived early the next day to meet with the therapist. She met him in the rehabilitation unit near the nurse's station. He noticed Sherry and came out of his office.

"Jane is progressing wonderfully. Her financial situation is yet to be resolved, but I do feel that she could benefit from further rehabilitation services. You are the only person that visits her so I wasn't sure where to turn." He said.

Where is she going to go?" Sherry asked.

"I have spoken with social services to find a suitable home for her." Sherry's heart sank. She was so used to having her right here nearby. This was devastating news, but she knew she should have known she couldn't stay here forever.

"Will she be sent to another rehab? A nursing home?" She asked.

"We believe she could benefit from further rehabilitation. She needs to learn to do things for herself, such as cooking, cleaning, taking her medicine and such."

"Is there a place close that can do that?"

"There is a nursing home that has a rehabilitation wing three miles from here. We believe she could benefit from what they have to offer." He smiled.

Sherry didn't know how to tell Jane but knew that she had to. She arrived at her room to find her working on a crossword puzzle book. Jane smiled the moment she seen her. Sherry sat down beside her to deliver the news.

"I am not good at giving bad news." Sherry started.

"What? What is it?" Jane asked.

"The hospital has decided to discharge you. They are sending you to a nursing home for further rehab."

Jane burst into tears and said, "No, no they cannot do that. I will never see you."

Sherry hugged her and said, "No that is not true. I will be there every day the same as here."

"Do you promise?"

"Yes." Sherry reassured her.

That evening, Sherry went home and grabbed her laptop. She wanted to learn more about Tommy. She googled his brother, Jake Hill of Phoenix, Arizona. Many references were available for arrest records. It seemed Jake had quite a bit of trouble with the law. Drug charges, Theft Charges and then the murder charge that finally got him the death sentence.

He was charged with killing a young girl from Phoenix at the time of the murder in January 1998, it appears the victim was 17 and Jake was 20. The story read:

"Jake Hill, 20 has been arrested for the murder of Stephanie Kramer, 17 of Phoenix, Arizona. It appears the motive was rape. The victim was found naked in a field on Saturday. She had been beaten and bludgeoned one day after she was reported missing. Jake Hill was found with her blood stained clothes in his car. Jake Hill is currently being held in the county jail on first degree murder charges."

The next article Sherry found read:

"Jake Hill, 20 of Phoenix has plead not guilty to first degree murder charges."

The last article she pulled up read:

"Jake Hill, 20 of Phoenix found guilty of first degree murder charges and sentenced to death in prison without parole."

She closed the laptop, not wanting to read any more about this creep. His mother said that he and Tommy were inseparable. She couldn't help, but wonder if Tommy had witnessed the incident and couldn't bare the trauma. Perhaps, he took his own life after watching what his brother had done to that poor girl. Sherry decided that the next opportunity that she had to get away for a day that she would pay Jake a visit. She decided that she also needed to pay Carl Lipton a visit. She knew that Josh would be mad if he learned of this, but she felt she had to follow through in finding out what happened to Tommy.

The next day, Sherry arrived to the hospital and found Jane packing her things. Jane seemed upset and said that they were discharging her that afternoon to Twin Pines Health and Rehab. Sherry assured her that she would be there as soon as her shift was over. Jane seemed very nervous about the coming change. Sherry hugged her.

"I understand that you are scared. I would be too. Jane, you are going to get through this. It's only temporary and I will be there every day I promise." Sherry smiled.

Jane nodded, wiping her tears and said, "Do you promise?"

Sherry hugged her and said, "I promise."

She was packed and gone within a matter of a few minutes. They transported her in a small bus. Sherry waved as they drove away fighting back her own tears. That evening at work, she felt like a nervous mother that had left her children with a sitter for the first time. She kept fighting the urge to call and check on Jane.

Once her shift ended, she drove directly to the nursing home, anxious to see Jane. The nurse pointed to her room and asked that she quietly enter as to not disturb the other residents. She opened the door and noted Jane awake right away lying in the bed. Sherry turned to find the light switch and flipped the light on. Jane sat up on the side of the bed dangling her feet off the side. Sherry turned on the light on then turned to note her sitting with her back to her.

"Jane, I'm here. I told you I would come straight over." Sherry announced.

"Who is Jane? Tommy doesn't know anyone named Jane. Momma said that Tommy is a good boy and she loves Tommy. I miss my Momma." Jane's voice was deep and strong. She spoke with a distinct country accent.

"Tommy, do you know where you are?" Sherry asked.

"It's dark, very dark. Tommy doesn't like the dark. Momma always leaves a light on for Tommy. Where is Jake? Jake won't like them being mean to Tommy." Jane began to fall forward.

Sherry grabbed her and leaned her back on the bed. Jane opened her beautiful blue eyes.

"What happened to me?" Jane asked.

Sherry nodding her head said, "Nothing Jane, nothing."

"I keep having these episodes where I feel like I am not me. It feels like I lose time or something. Do you think there is something wrong with me?" She had a fear in her eyes that Sherry had never seen.

"Jane, there is nothing wrong with you. You're fine." Sherry helped her get re-situated in her bed. She tucked her in and tried to make small talk about her new temporary home. Although, she seemed perplexed throughout the visit.

Sherry left there even more determined to piece this puzzle together. She felt as if Jane deserved a normal life and it could never be had as long as Tommy was tormenting her. She had so many unanswered questions in her mind and she knew my next visit would have to be to Mr. Lipton. That evening Joe and Sherry had a great dinner.

"You haven't been speaking much of Jane lately." Joe said.

"She is progressing very fast and they moved her to a new rehab today. It's only three miles from the hospital and I visited her after work tonight."

"When will she be able to go out on visits?"

"Wow, I hadn't even thought about that. I could ask tomorrow. That would be wonderful if she could come here for a visit and meet you."

"That would be great. Find out tomorrow and let me know. We can plan a dinner out and it will be my treat."

"I know she would love that." Sherry giggled.

The next evening when Sherry stopped by to visit Jane, she was sitting up watching television in the chair next to her bed. She seemed anxious to see Sherry.

"Sherry, how long do you think I will have to stay here?" Sherry sat beside her.

"I have no idea, but the therapist at the hospital said that you were progressing quickly." Sherry replied.

Jane looked to the ceiling, appearing to fight back tears and said, "I think that there is something wrong with me. It's very hard to explain, but sometimes I feel as if I am not me. It's like I am somebody else. I know that sounds crazy. Do you think I am crazy?"

Sherry reached over and hugged her.

"I do not think you are crazy, because if you are crazy, then I must be crazy too."

"Why do you say that?" Jane smiled.

"Well I cannot explain that right now. I did however bring a game of checkers and thought I might beat you in a couple of games after we go grab a soda from the vending machine."

"We will see about that. I recall winning the last several games." Jane laughed. They stopped by the nurse's office and asked about her being able to leave on passes.

"I will check with the administrator and let you know tomorrow." The nurse said. Sherry was her only listed contact and felt confident that they would agree.

Sherry awoke to her phone ringing early the next morning.

"Hello." Sherry answered the call.

The lady on the other end said, "Hello. This is Dina Sharp at Twin Pines Health and Rehab. I have spoken with the administrator and he has agreed that passes can be allowed for Miss Jane Smith. He encourages that she be returned before 8 in the evening and no more than four hour leaves."

"That is wonderful. Thank you for calling." Sherry said and hung up the phone. She rolled over, smiling at Joe.

"Was that a yes on the passes from the home for Jane?" Joe asked.

"Yes." She said, smiling.

"Great. I am off this Friday and I believe you are too. We have a date. I am taking two beautiful women to dinner."

"You better not be flirting with my best friend." Sherry giggled.

"And what if I do?" He laughed.

"I will kick your ass." He started tickling her as she fought him off.

Sherry couldn't wait to give Jane the news. She was anxious all day awaiting the moment she could clock out and rush to her. She arrived to find Jane playing with the crossword puzzle book. Sherry was beaming with joy as she entered the room. Jane noticed it right away.

"Wow. Did you win the lottery?" Jane asked.

Sherry danced over beside her, sat down and said, "I feel like I did."

Jane turned to her inquisitively.

"The home here as agreed to let you leave with me on passes." Sherry announced.

Jane immediately began to beam with joy. She covered her mouth with both hands and tried to hide her open smile.

"What?" Jane said with excitement.

"That is right, we are going out Friday night. Joe is taking us to dinner."

Jane was so excited she was speechless. Sherry knew she didn't have anything to wear. Sherry had decided to do some shopping early on in case things didn't fit. They spent the week trying on clothes after work and finally settled on a pair of black slacks and a red button up blouse. Jane looked beautiful, she had a natural beauty about her. She didn't require make-up of fancy hairdos she was naturally pretty. She was tiny in stature and only after trying several sizes did I come to realize that size one fit her best. Sherry was 5'10 and often felt like a giant next to her. Jane was five foot and tiny, this often gave Sherry the mental imprint that Jane was a child.

Sherry insisted that Joe accompany her to meet Jane Friday night. He was reluctant but finally agreed. Sherry was so excited that she could hardly bare the drive over. They arrived to find her dressed and waiting. Sherry introduced Jane to Joe.

"I finally get to meet this mysterious man that I have heard so much about." Jane said.

"I have heard about you as well since the day the two of you met. It is a true pleasure to meet you." Joe smiled.

"Thank you. It is a pleasure to meet you as well." She turned to grab her small purse that Sherry had bought for her and suddenly she appeared unstable.

Sherry quickly ran to her and grabbed her. Jane slowly sat down with Sherry's assistance.

"Jane are you okay?" Sherry asked.

"Yes, I am fine. I just got dizzy for a minute. It must be all of the excitement, I am fine." She tried to stand back up and was dizzy again. Sitting back down, she said," I don't know what has come over me. I felt fine." Jane had tears in her eyes.

"Let me get the nurse in here." Sherry insisted.

"I will go get you some water." Joe offered.

"I wanted to go. Just once, I wanted to go somewhere and feel like I mattered." Jane cried.

Sherry began to cry as well once Jane said that.

"Now listen, this was by no means a one time offer. I can go get a pizza and we can play games instead tonight. We can go out another time." Joe said.

Sherry smiled at his ability to smooth things over so quickly.

"That would be great. Joe, you go get the pizza and I will set up the game." Sherry said.

Jane was still crying as he left the room. The nurse came in checked her vitals and dismissed the incident as being too much excitement.

They played checkers, Monopoly and Sorry for several hours. Jane laughed at many of Joes corny jokes and seemed to enjoy the night. He waited outside the door as Sherry helped her into the bed.

"I had a good time anyway, I want you to know that." Jane smiled.

Sherry smiled and said, "I did too."

"I guess that's why they say that." Jane said.

"Say what?"

"I heard it on TV the other day. They said, "'If life gives you lemons, make lemonade.'"

"This is a perfect example." Sherry giggled.

She tucked her in and kissed her forehead. Sherry was exiting the door with her hand on the light switch.

"Sherry." Jane said softly.

Sherry stopped and looked toward her.

"Thank you." Jane nodded.

"No, thank you."

Sherry left the rehab for the evening and headed back to her home with Joe.

"I am so sorry that this night didn't work out the way you had planned." Joe said as he was driving.

"It's not your fault. Besides, you saved the day. You have this fantastic ability to make everything okay no matter the circumstances." She smiled.

"So does that mean that you're going to thank me when we get home?" Joe smirked.

"Maybe."

"I better drive faster."

She laughed again as he seemed to lean forward, speed up and focus on the road intently.

They made love and it was wonderful as always. She wondered how she could be so lucky as to find the best man on the planet. He was perfect, tall and handsome. She was too tall and often clumsy. She had wide hips and short hair that seemed to stay at a length that was either too short for a pony tail and too long to style. He insisted that she was beautiful and would tell her daily.

She still felt guilty about keeping the Tommy Hill secret from him. She kept telling herself that if she gathered enough information, she would share it with him. She even had imagined him helping her solve the case.

The next morning, Sherry woke up thinking about Tommy Hill. She had so many questions running through her mind and was eager to find out what was going on with Jane.

"Joe?" Sherry said.

"Yes, Beautiful."

"Do you ever remember hearing about a man named Jake Hill?"

He sat straight up in the bed and said, "Why are you asking?"

"A patient came in last week. He was babbling about Jake Hill. He was saying he killed a girl and was a cold blooded murderer."

Joe leaned back on the bed and put his hand on his forehead. He sighed, then said, "Jake Hill was a sick bastard. I was a teenager when he killed that girl. Everyone knew he was crazy, but we didn't know just how crazy until he did that."

"Do you remember him having a brother?"

"No, why?" Joe asked.

"I thought that he had said something about Jake having a brother that disappeared."

Josh got out of the bed and dismissed their conversation. He said, "I never knew of him having a brother."

She was off the next day and planned on trying to contact Mr. Lipton. She checked the phone book and his name surfaced right away. His address was given as 1432 King Street in Phoenix. She checked a google map search and determined it was minutes from the hospital. She rehearsed her speech repeatedly in her mind as she made the drive.

The house was a large brick home, well maintained with a perfectly manicured lawn. She noted a vehicle in the driveway and lights on inside. She made her way to the porch and rang the bell. A woman in her sixties with perfect hair and make-up wearing a blue polyester pant suit answered the door.

"Can I help you?" The woman inquisitively asked.

"Yes, ma'am I was hoping to speak with Mr. Lipton." Sherry replied.

"What is this regarding?"

"A case that he handled a long time ago. I wanted to ask some questions."

"Oh dear. Mr. Lipton doesn't live here anymore."

Sherry felt sudden devastation and said, "Where does he live?"

"Dear, I am afraid he has Alzheimer's. He hasn't been well for quite some time. He is at Twin Pines Health and Rehab."

"I am so sorry to have bothered you ma'am. Can I ask you one more question?"

"I will answer if I can." The woman said.

"Did you ever hear him speak of a case regarding Tommy Hill?"

She lost her smile right away and said, "Please, come in."

Sherry entered into a perfectly organized, clean beautiful home. Not a thing out of place. The carpet appeared to have never been walked on and the furniture appeared new. She directed her into the kitchen where her china sparkled in her mahogany china cabinet. She offered tea and Sherry accepted.

Once the tea was ready, the woman poured each of them a cup and sat down across from Sherry. She seemed to study Sherry's face for a moment.

"That was one of the worst cases that Carl ever had to suffer through. You see, Tommy was the brother to the boy that killed Carl's best friend's daughter. When Jake killed that girl, it destroyed Carl's partner Bill Kramer." She stirred her tea and then said, "Bills only daughter was gone in the blink of an eye. She was brutally murdered and for no reason. When they found her bloody and clothes in Jake's car, the whole town wanted to tear him limb from limb.

Bill and Carl had been partners and friends for over a decade so it felt like family to Carl. A few weeks later, when Mrs. Hill reported Tommy missing, it seemed that Carl couldn't take it seriously. He tried to do his job. He was a good man, but deep down inside, it pained him to do it."

"Why didn't he step down and let another officer take the case?" Sherry asked.

"He didn't want to seem weak I suppose."

"Did he ever look for Tommy?"

"That is not a question I can answer. I never asked and he never talked about it." She sighed and said, "Only Carl can answer that. Well, unfortunately he can't now."

"And Bill? What happened to him?" Sherry asked.

"Bill couldn't live with the pain. He took his own life just months after his daughter was murdered. His wife is still alive and she lives somewhere near here. I see her every now and then at the grocery store."

"What is her name?"

"Katherine, Katherine Masters. You see, Stephanie was an illegitimate child. Her mother and father were never married."

"Masters? Are you sure?" Sherry asked.

"Yes, dear. Masters."

"Thank you!" Sherry nodded and started walking toward the front door.

"Dear, please leave me your phone number."

Sherry wrote her number quickly on a napkin and left.

She sat in her car, trying to catch her breath and digest the information she had been handed. Her heart was pounding, her mind was racing. How could this be? Joe had never spoken to her about a family member being murdered. Was this a coincidence? The name, was it coincidence? She wasn't sure what to do. Should she call and ask Joe? Should she stop investigating and never speak a word of what she had learned?

She drove to Twin Pines in a daze. Her head was spinning as she was still trying to process all the new information. Once she entered the building, the nurse smiled.

"Jane is awake. She is watching television. She will be pleased to see you." The nurse said.

"Actually, I want to inquire about a different patient. Carl, Carl Lipton?" Sherry asked.

44

"Mr. Lipton is here." The nurse nodded, "Would you like me to direct you to his room?"

"Please." Sherry followed her down a long hallway until it ended. They took a right, and walked to the last room on the right. The nurse pointed at the door.

"This is it. I hope you didn't come with plans of speaking with him. He hasn't spoken a word since he arrived." The nurse said.

Sherry knocked on the door as she peaked in and noted him sitting in a Geri chair with his back to the door.

"Mr. Lipton?" Sherry called out. He didn't respond. She walked to face him. His face was much older than a man of his age.

It appeared that time had taken its toll on him. His eyes were cloudy as if cataracts had eaten their way to his brain. His head had a constant shake as if the nerves were destroyed. He was thin and pale, with skin of leather. His skin was thin and appeared taped back together in several places along his arms and hands. His mouth was closed yet he donned a constant chewing motion.

"Mr. Lipton you do not know me, but I am here about Tommy Hill." Sherry said.

He raised his head to look at her. The name meant something to him.

"I guess that woke you up?" Sherry said. He looked down again. She said, "I only have one question." He continued to stare at the floor. "Why didn't you investigate his disappearance?"

He swallowed then raised his head. He opened his mouth to show his yellowed broken teeth and reached for her with his right hand. Yelling as loud as he could as if in a fit of anger. She jumped back as the nurse came in.

45

"What happened?" The nurse asked.

Sherry smiled and said, "I have no idea. I was just speaking to him when he suddenly became enraged."

The nurse asked her to step outside as she checked on him. She left the room and within a few minutes the nurse emerged.

"I think it's best that you say your goodbyes for the day." The nurse said.

Sherry watched as she walked away. She stepped back in the room.

"I do have one more question for you." She paused then walked closer to Carl. "Are you here because of guilt or karma?"

He raised his head again. She turned to walk away. As she approached the door, Carl mumbled, "That fat bastard deserved whatever he got."

She stopped and turned back toward him then said, "Perhaps you did too." She could still hear him yelling as she continued to walk.

Sherry was still shaken up when she arrived at Jane's room. Jane must have sensed it.

"Sherry, are you okay? You look like you've seen a ghost." Jane asked.

"Oh, I am fine. It's nothing really." Sherry replied.

"It doesn't look like nothing."

"Let's take a walk. Maybe we can go outside and get some fresh air?"

Jane quickly grabbed her shoes and cane. They walked to the benches outside under the tree.

"It's almost ironic that I am trying to help you find out who you are and instead, find out that someone else is not who I thought they were." Sherry said.

"What do you mean?" Jane asked.

"Someday we are going to have a long talk about that, but not today." Sherry said and then changed the topic. "Listen this coming Saturday I am off. Joe is going on another hunting expedition and I have a friend that lives near the bottom of the mountain. She is an elderly woman that lives by herself. I was thinking about driving over and paying a visit. Perhaps you would like to join me? I think you would like her."

"That would be awesome." Jane smiled.

"Then it is set, we are going. I will be by to get you at 8am."

"I will be ready by 8." Jane nodded.

Sherry didn't want Joe to suspect anything so she cooked a nice dinner and awaited his arrival. It was going to be difficult for her to keep all of this to herself.

"Wow, you're getting pretty damn good at this cooking and cleaning stuff. Keep it up and I might have to keep you." Joe said as he walked into the kitchen.

Sherry smiled and kissed him. They made small talk about his job mostly. He liked to tell her stories about dumb criminals. Some of his stories were pretty funny.

"Joe, on Saturday when I am off, I am taking Jane for a drive to the mountain. She hasn't been there before and I figured since you are working anyway it would be a nice day."

"That is a great idea. I am sure she will enjoy it. The scenery is absolutely beautiful up there." Joe said.

"Great, I should be home before you are and we can go out to eat if you want?"

"Sounds to me like someone is trying to get out of cooking again." Joe laughed.

"Maybe" Sherry said sarcastically.

Saturday morning came and Sherry was anxious. She wasn't sure what she had hoped to gain out of taking Jane to visit Mrs. Hill but felt it necessary. It was going to be over 100 degrees today. She was packing water bottles as Joe left for work. He honked and yelled out the window, "Bye, beautiful." As he drove away.   Sherry arrived at Twin Pines at exactly 8am. Jane was dressed and ready as promised. She smiled as Sherry walked into the room. She was wearing one of the sweat suits that Sherry had bought for her.

"Jane, it is supposed to be over 100 degrees today. I think you better change into shorts and a t-shirt." Sherry laughed.

"Now you tell me." Jane smirked. She quickly went into the restroom to change when the nurse came for Sherry to sign the pass.

The nurse waited for Jane to finish changing and then handed her pills for the day to take in front of her. Jane quickly swallowed them down then opened her mouth to show her empty tongue.

"Now that's attractive." Sherry said. The nurse laughed and shook her head. They were on the highway within 30 minutes.

"What kind of music do you prefer?" Sherry said as she fiddled with the radio.

"I don't know." Jane looked confused.

"Let's find out." Sherry said, smiling.

She tried Country, Rock, and Pop.

"I think I prefer Country." Jane proclaimed.

"Country it is." Sherry said as she adjusted the channel.

Jane was leaning on the window only 30 minutes into the drive and fell asleep. She probably was too anxious to sleep last night. Sherry thought.

As they exited off the highway to take the short drive to the Hill house, Jane suddenly sat up and said, "Tommy lives near her. Tommy is going to see his momma." In the man's voice.

Sherry was startled and quickly pulled the car to the side of the road. With her heart racing she said, "That is right. Tommy is going to see his momma. Tommy's momma loves Tommy. She says that Tommy is a good boy and Tommy's momma misses Tommy too."

"Let's go please, Tommy wants to see his momma." Jane said.

Sherry pulled the car back on the road and proceeded toward the house. She was pulling in front of the house when Jane went limp and fell back against the window. Sherry shook her to wake her, she opened her eyes and said.

"I'm sorry. I must have dozed off." Jane looked out the window and said, "Is this your friend's house?"

"Yes it is, let's get out and go in."

Sherry had called Mrs. Hill earlier in the week and said that she would be coming by with some fresh baked bread and promised not to speak of Tommy. Mrs. Hill had said that she welcomed the company.

Mrs. Hill had heard them pull up and was standing on the porch watching as they emerged from the vehicle. Sherry quickly grabbed the bread from the backseat and helped Jane maneuver through her muddy driveway. She invited them in as Sherry introduced her to Jane. Jane seemed taken by Mrs. Hill right away. She was immediately infatuated with the small Chihuahua and began playing with him. Yo-Yo seemed to be taken with her too rather quickly. He barked and growled at Sherry. He allowed Jane to pet on him right away.

Mrs. Hill seemed to enjoy the company and Jane's many questions regarding the photos decorating the room. Mrs. Hill showed Jane many of her handmade quilts. Jane complimented her on her skills and Mrs. Hill quickly offered to teach her sewing. As they were preparing to leave, Mrs. Hill said, "Now, hold on one minute." She darted off down the hall. She came back and handed Jane a small matchbox car.

"Tommy loved these little cars like this. He had his favorite with him when he disappeared, always kept it in his pocket." Mrs. Hill said as she handed it to Jane.

Jane looked at the small car and her face lit up.

"I'm going to keep this with me all the time for good luck. Thank you so much." Jane said.

Sherry promised them both that they would come back. They spent a couple of hours at Mrs. Hills house then had to say their goodbyes and head home. They left with the promise of a return. Mrs. Hill never seemed to notice Jane's right foot was the same as hers and neither did Jane.

The drive home seemed shorter than the drive there. Sherry left there feeling as if she had done the right thing. She wasn't sure however, why it was the right thing. She hoped that Tommy had been able to see his mother and know that she was okay. Jane stayed awake the entire drive back. They stopped by a small diner and had lunch then drove back to Twin Pines. Jane thanked her for the afternoon several times. Jane spent most of the drive back about how wonderful Mrs. Hill was. She was elated that she had made another friend. She was also glad that Mrs. Hill had made a new friend.

When Sherry arrived home, Joe was already there. She was curious as to why he would be home so early. She walked in to find him sitting on the couch drinking a beer. He seen her and finished what was left in the can then crushed the can.

"Joe, Is everything okay?" Sherry asked.

"I don't know, you tell me. Is everything okay?" As he grabbed another can of beer from the refrigerator.

"What are you talking about?" Sherry asked.

"Well, apparently you have been snooping around. Rumor has it that you paid Mrs. Lipton a visit. She said that you were asking questions about the disappearance of Tommy Hill. They say you went to the nursing home and paid Carl Lipton a visit as well. Is this true?"

"Joe, wait a minute. I can explain."

He grabbed her throat and began to squeeze then said, "No, no you can't. Do you hear me? You can't explain. Now I want to know where all of this came from. Does Jane the retard have something to do with this?"

Sherry was shaking her head, eyes wide, mouthing the word, "No." He took his hand off her neck then struck the refrigerator with his fist behind her head.

"People around here tend to get upset when outsiders stick their nose where it doesn't belong." He sighed then said, "I love you, but I don't want to hear another word about you snooping around. Do you hear me?"

51

Sherry nodded.

He said louder, "Do you hear me? Answer me."

"Yes, yes I hear you."

He stormed out the front door, got into his police cruiser and drove away. Sherry steadied herself trying to catch her breath. She had never seen a violent side to Joe. She had never expected that he had one. That was a different man altogether than the one she had married. She felt confident that his family was tied up in this mess somehow, but still wasn't sure how.

Joe would have been a teenager at that time she thought. Perhaps, near the murdered girl's age. She had met his parents only once before. They lived in Tucson but moved only five years ago from here. They seemed like nice people. His father was a retired police captain and his mother was a retired school teacher. He has one sister that lives in California. She recalled her as being younger than Joe.

She hoped that he wouldn't return for the rest of the evening. She was shaken over his outburst and didn't feel safe with him. She slept listening intently for any sign of his arrival.

The next morning when she awoke, she noted he was not in the bed. She quietly made her way into the living room to find he wasn't there either. She breathed a sigh of relief to find he hadn't come home.

She decided that she should call in a sick day at work. She was too shaken up over what had happened and knew he would be home soon. She wanted to be gone when he did arrive so she quickly got dressed. She grabbed a few things in a small bag, mostly things she couldn't bear to lose. She made her way to the car. As she was driving away, she noticed a note on her car windshield under the wiper blade.

She drove slowly to a side road before stopping. She stepped out and grabbed the note. She laid it on the seat next to her then proceeded on. She wanted to be completely out of the neighborhood before stopping for anything.

Once she had reached a larger more populated side of town she located a motel and rented a room. She made her way to her room then realized that she had left the note in the seat. She quickly ran back, grabbed it, and then locked herself in the room. She anxiously opened the note. It read:

I am writing this note to let you know that you are putting yourself in a very dangerous situation. If you continue to snoop into this, you will be dealt with. I also tried to investigate this crime years ago and it led to me having to leave and go into hiding. If you want more information please contact me at 602-555-9645.

She put the phone number in her contacts in her phone and saved it. Using the contact name "unknown". She took the piece of paper and tore it into many pieces then flushed it down the toilet. She was unsure if she should trust whomever this was. She thought it could be a setup. She laid down to take a nap. She awoke to her phone ringing. She grabbed her phone and noted it was Joe on the caller ID.

"Hello." She answered the phone.

"Babe, listen, we need to talk." Joe said on the other line. She didn't reply. There was a brief pause of silence.

"I'm sorry. I really am, I want to talk to you." Joe pleaded.

"I will have to think about it."

"Please, just give me a chance. I really need to talk to you. Please, we can meet somewhere in a public place if you want. I really need to talk to you."

"Meet me at the cafeteria in the hospital in two hours." Sherry replied.

"Okay, I will be there."

She hung up.

She arrived 30 minutes early and was sipping her coffee when he arrived. He looked disheveled and tired. He sat down across from her as she watched intensely. He had already gotten himself a cup of coffee and was shaking as he placed it on the table. He peered into her eyes.

"I'm sorry. I have no idea what came over me. I wish I could take it all back but I can't." Joe said.

"I want the truth. I want you to tell me the truth." Sherry demanded. The only thing that she wanted to hear was the truth.

"I don't know what you are talking about. This town had many upstanding police officers back then and still does. Let them do their job and leave it alone." Joe shook his head.

"I can't."

He gazed at her with grave eyes and said, "What does Jane have to do with this?"

"Nothing. This has absolutely nothing to do with Jane."

He leaned back in his chair with a sly expression and said, "I don't believe you. I think that retard does have something to do with it and I intend to find out."

"Then I guess we both have our work cut out for us." She shrugged her shoulders. She stood up to walk away when he suddenly grabbed her arm and pulled her in toward him.

"People get hurt, everyday people disappear and are never found. It would be a shame if something were to happen to you or someone that you care about." Joe threatened.

She yanked her arm free and said, "It would also be a shame if corrupt police officers were to be exposed." As she stormed away from the table.

Her mind was still racing when she got into her car. She was sitting in the driver seat trying to gather her thoughts when she saw another note on her windshield. She stepped out to grab it then quickly stepped back into the car and locked her doors. It was folded four ways, the same as the other one. She unfolded it and began to read:

You are in grave danger. I have been exactly where you are in this investigation. The Phoenix police will not be exposed for their corruption. You must contact me so that we can discuss matters safely. Your life depends on it. 602-555-9645.

She tore the note into many pieces as she gazed about. She noted a security guard in a post with binoculars aimed toward her. She quickly started her car and proceeded out of the parking lot. She drove back to her motel room and flushed the note down the toilet. She laid down and cried for several hours. She had a perfect life a few days ago. She had everything that any woman could want. It was hard for me to believe that this had happened this fast. She wanted to take it back as well, but knew that she couldn't. She knew that she owed it to both Jane and Tommy to find out what happened.

She dozed off and when she awoke, it was dark outside. She glanced at her phone to check the time. It was 8:14. She had missed work and not called. She called and asked to speak with her supervisor. She was put on hold for several minutes when he answered.

"Sherry, it seems that you didn't call or show up today. It appears that this is probably not a suitable position for you. The hospital believes it would be in our best interest if you seek employment elsewhere. Good luck." The supervisor hung up.

She had worked there for two years and had never missed, came in late or been reprimanded. She was shaking her head in shock, wondering why they would fire her without even speaking with her first.

She lay back on the bed, staring at the ceiling when she picked up her phone and searched her contacts for "Unknown". She nervously clicked the call button. It rang twice when a man answered.

"Hello." He said.

She sat up and said, "This is Sherry, Sherry Masters."

"I have been waiting for your call. We must meet but not in Phoenix or anywhere near there. Can you come to Mesa?" He asked.

"I can in the morning."

"Call me when you get here. We will arrange a meeting place."

"Wait? Who is this?" Sherry asked.

"Not now. We will discuss that when we meet."

"Okay." The phone call ended at that.

She drove to Mesa the next morning. She left before daylight in fear of being followed. She pulled into a small diner and went inside to order coffee. Once she was seated and sipping coffee, she called "Unknown." It rang twice and he answered.

"Hello." The man answered.

"I'm here."

"Great. Meet me at Buds Diner on Grand in an hour."

Okay."

She finished her coffee and using google maps, she was at Buds in less than 20 minutes. She went inside and ordered a coffee. She waited patiently, pondering how he would know who she was. Her phone rang again with the contact shown "Unknown." She nervously answered.

"Hello." Sherry said into the phone.

"I am going to walk through the door in 30 seconds."

She turned to watch the door and noted a tall man in his late thirties walked into the diner. He was wearing a baseball cap that was red. He had on cowboy boots and tight jeans. A stylish western shirt that was tucked in to expose his large western belt buckle. His hair was very short and complexion dark. She waved as he sprinted toward her.

He sat across from her and said, "I'm David Keller. You must think I am crazy."

"No." Sherry nodded.

"I have a friend that works with the Phoenix police department. I told him that if anything ever surfaced again regarding the disappearance of Tommy Hill, that I wanted to know about it." He sighed and said, "He called me last week and said that he had noticed the case file pulled. He said that your husband was pulled into the captain's office with it."

"Do you know what happened to Tommy Hill?" Sherry asked.

He shook his head and said, "No. My father was on the Phoenix Police force when Tommy Disappeared. He felt as if things were not being handled properly and made the mistake of voicing his opinion. I was only a teenager at the time. My father was shot and killed in a suspicious crime within weeks of Tommy disappearing. I couldn't let it rest. I went back a few years ago and started asking questions about the disappearance of Tommy Hill. Within a day of my arrival I was threatened and made to leave."

"How did you find out that I was asking questions about it?"

"My friend at the department called and told me that Mrs. Lipton called and said that you visited her. She said that you paid her a visit and were asking questions about it."

"Do you know if Mrs. Lipton was informing the department or your friend? That makes a difference."

He stared at her for a minute then said, "The department."

"I have lost everything over this. My husband, my job, and everything has changed in a matter of days." Sherry shook her head.

"I'm sorry, but if you are not careful, you could lose your life. This is a very dangerous situation." He warned.

"I guess you expect me to walk away from it? I am supposed to get up and walk away as if I didn't find any of this out?"

"I can't tell you what to do. I can tell you that if you continue to ask questions and dig into it, you could be killed."

She nodded as she glared out the window.

"I wanted more than anything to find out what happened. It haunts me still that I couldn't find out who killed my father." He said.

"Okay, thanks for the warning." She grabbed my purse to leave.

He reached over and took her hand into his, then gazed into her eyes and said, "I would love to help you. I would love to find out what happened to my father. I'm not sure what to do. Listen, if you get any information that can help, then call me. I am an attorney here. If you get anything worth reopening it with the state police then please let me know."

Sherry nodded.

"One more thing I should mention. While I was there investigating I came across something."

"What?"

"I have noted that since before Stephanie and Tommy, to this day, a girl seems to go missing at least once or twice a year. The only similarities are that the girls are always handicapped in one way or another. I don't think Jake Hill killed that girl. I know he was a crazy drug addict." He nodded his head and continued, "I don't think he killed that girl though."

"Why do you say that?" Sherry asked.

"Because you wouldn't kill someone then drive around with their clothes and blood in your car and not dispose of it. They found the evidence in his trunk. He probably didn't even know it was there."

Sherry nodded and said, "Thank you for your time."

"Please, if I can help, do not hesitate to call." She walked away Feeling as if she had gained nothing.

Chapter 3

She fought back tears as she drove back toward Phoenix. Mrs. Hill's house was along the way and she decided to stop by and pay one more visit. She arrived to find her sitting on the porch alone. She smiled and waved as Sherry parked along the street. She seemed pleased to have a visitor. Sherry suspected she spent most days alone.

As Sherry approached the house, Mrs. Hill said, "I'll go get you a glass of ice tea."

Sherry smiled, then sat down on the porch swing next to her rocker. She was back wielding a huge glass of iced tea.

"It is hotter than Hades today." Mrs. Hill proclaimed.

"I hope you don't mind the unexpected visit." Sherry smiled.

"You're welcome anytime. Why didn't Jane come along?"

"I am on my way back from somewhere else and thought I would stop by on my way home."

After a few moments, Sherry said, "I am going to be honest with you Mrs. Hill."

"I know you want to ask me something so just ask."

"It's about Tommy." Sherry sighed and continued, "Do you remember if Tommy had any friends or acquaintances besides Jake?"

"Tommy had several friends. Tommy was in special classes at school. Most of the kids in there were slow like him. He had four or five kids he was friends with. There was one girl that he really liked."

"Do you remember her name?"

"Of course. It's the girl that Jake was accused of killing. Stephanie Kramer. I guess that is why Tommy took it so hard when they accused his brother of killing her." She shook her head and continued, "Jake might not have been the best kid in town, but he didn't kill that girl."

"Tell me about Stephanie." Sherry said.

"She was the nicest little girl. You see, her mother was a drunk and had an affair with one of the cops here in town. His name was Bill Kramer. He denied she was his at first. Probably because her mother slept with anybody that would fund her habit. Later when they proved Stephanie was Bill's, he didn't have a choice but to accept her as his own. He loved her more than life itself after that. Stephanie was born a slow learner. I suspect it was due to her mother's drinking habits. Stephanie was never bigger than a minute. She wasn't never bigger than most 10 year olds."

"How did Jake feel about Stephanie?"

"Jake loved her like a sister. He would even play games with her and Tommy. Her Mother would drop her off here and leave her for the day. Stephanie was like one of the family. I felt as if she was the daughter I never had." She leaned in toward Sherry and said, "You know, Jane reminds me a lot of Stephanie. I reckon that's why I took such a liking to her."

"The night that Stephanie went missing, do you know where Jake and Tommy were?"

"Tommy went to a dance at school. He was dressed up like a million bucks. Jake was going to drop Tommy off and then go see his girlfriend, Lynn."

"Lynn?" Sherry asked.

"Jake had a girlfriend, but I never particularly care for her. She wasn't nothing but trouble. She smoked, cussed and had tattoos all over her. She was always getting that boy in trouble. I tried to tell him that she wasn't no good but he wouldn't listen."

"Do you remember her last name?"

"Brooks, Lynn Brooks."

"Do you know where she is now?"

Mrs. Hill shook her head and said, "No. I never heard a word out of her after Jake got arrested. I reckon she never visited him either. She wasn't no good."

"Do you know where she lived?"

"She lived right up the road." She pointed and said, "You can't miss it, the house with the broken swing set in the front yard. There is an old rusty silo around back that you can see from the road. I believe her momma still lives there."

"Were there any other friends that visited Tommy or Jake?"

"Jake had a best friend that practically lived here. They were close as brothers. He still comes by to check on me. He was just here the other day."

"What's his name?"

"Walter, Walter Jones. He is a mechanic and works for Reins auto repair. He is a good boy. He was a troubled kid like Jake but he is a good boy now. He comes by at least once a week to check on me. He almost always brings food. I reckon he's worried I might starve." Mrs. Hill said, laughing.

Sherry could see the pain in her eyes. As she laughed, her belly bounced up and down as if she forced it. She had clothes pins in her pockets on her house dress. Safety pins held the pockets in place. She had three dresses on the clothes line that hung steady on the line without even a whisper of a breeze in the brawling sun. I assumed she was on the porch since her house only had a small box fan in the living room. The heat was unrelenting this year. Today was expected to be over 100 again.

They spent a good part of the afternoon talking. Mrs. Hill enjoyed the company or at least Sherry felt as if she did. Sherry wanted to help her anyway she could. Sherry left more determined than ever to find out what really happened to Tommy Hill.

She drove a mile down the road when she noted the house with the broken swing set in the front yard. She then noted the rust silo in the back. There was a car in the yard. She honked and noted an older woman come to the door. The woman stepped out on the porch and motioned at Sherry to come in. Sherry smiled as she walked toward her.

The woman smiled back and said, "Can I help you with something?"

"I hope so." Sherry sighed due to the heat and said, "I'm looking for Lynn Brooks."

She shook her head and her disposition quickly changed. She was now sarcastically replying, "Seems a lot of people are looking for Lynn these days."

"Why do you say that?" Sherry sheepishly said.

"A man came by the other day and was wanting to talk to her. I'll tell you the same thing I told him." She turned to look toward the sky then back at Sherry as she said, "Lynn has changed. She is not partying, troubled, and dope smoking kid she used to be. She is good now. She got married and she is trying to move on. Kind of hard for her to do that with all of you people still wanting to ask questions."

"I'm sorry to have bothered you. Does Lynn still live around here?" Sherry smiled.

She nodded and said, "Yes, she does."

"The truth is, I am not a cop, and I am a nurse. I'm an unemployed nurse now as a matter of fact. I stumbled upon some information I wish now that I hadn't. I am simply trying to help some friends." Sherry explained.

"What's your name?"

"Sherry Masters."

She stepped back and said, "I'm guessing now that you married that Joe Masters boy."

"Yes, Why?" Sherry asked.

"That boy always thought he was above the law. Ran around here thinking he was better than everybody. He thought he owned this town. His family were mostly cops so it didn't matter what he did, they would fix it. He picked on poor old Tommy Hill and the rest of the handicapped kids. He made fun of everybody that didn't have money. I am sorry, but you will figure out that you made a huge mistake marrying that boy."

"I think I'm already figuring that out." Sherry nodded.

"What is it that you are looking for?"

"Honestly ma'am, I don't know. But, I feel like something isn't right about the disappearance Of Tommy Hill."

"There was a lot of things that were wrong about his disappearance. Mostly the fact that the cops didn't care. They didn't even look for him. His poor momma lost both of her boys. I never believed Jake killed that girl either. He was good to that little girl. He treated her like a sister."

Sherry wiped the sweat off her head and said, "I think you're right. I want to find out the truth. Will you help me talk to Lynn?"

"You're treading on dangerous territory when you start snooping around like this." The woman shook her head.

"I know. I have already been warned. I am not going to give up though."

"You're a stubborn one too. Leave me your phone number. I will give it to Lynn. I won't promise you that she will call, but I will give it to her."

"Fair enough." She thanked her and walked back to her car, wondering if Lynn would call.

It was getting late and she needed to find a room for the night. She had decided that morning to take her things and find a new room, it felt safer that way. She was driving toward the outskirts of town when her phone rang.

"Hello." Sherry answered.

The person on the other line said, "Mrs. Masters?"

"Yes."

"This is Connie with Twin Pines health and rehab. There has been an incident involving Jane."

Sherry's heart began to pound as she said, "What do you mean an incident?"

"Early this morning, one of our residents from the Alzheimer's unit got free and came into Jane's room. He was choking her when the aides arrived in her room. She is okay but visibly shaken none the less. You are listed as her emergency contact so I felt the need to notify you."

"This patient that barged into her room and choked her. His name wouldn't happen to be Mr. Lipton would it?"

There was total silence for several seconds before the woman replied. "How did you know that ma'am?"

"I'm just lucky I guess. Thank you for the information. Please tell Jane that I'm on my way."

Sherry arrived to find Jane sobbing in her bed. Jane immediately beamed with joy when Sherry walked into her room. She hugged Sherry so tight that it felt she was going to break her bones.

"What happened?" Sherry asked.

Jane wiped her tears and said, "I was asleep. I woke up and he was choking me. I started kicking the footboard. I couldn't scream. Luckily, someone heard the sounds of me kicking and rushed in."

"Listen Jane, listen closely. We have to get you out of here. I cannot explain right now but I will. I promise I will. You must act as if you are okay and want to take a ride to get out for a little while. Do you understand me?"

Jane nodded and said, "Okay."

Sherry called for the nurse.

"Can I help you?" The nurse asked.

"Yes, Jane and I are going to go out for ice cream."

The nurse looked at Jane and said, "Do you feel well enough right now?"

Jane nodded and said, "Yes, Ice cream always makes me feel better."

They grabbed what they could of her things. They shoved the belongings into Sherry's handbag and were driving away within minutes. They drove toward Mesa at a normal speed, not wanting to draw attention to themselves. They arrived in Mesa at dark. Sherry could sense the fear in Jane as she had hardly spoke a word since they left. They went into a Motel 6 and rented a room. They pulled around to the room that was located on the back side.

"I am scared that something bad has happened." Jane said.

Sherry turned to look at her child like face and said, "Jane, I am going to explain everything to you. I promise I am. Right now we need to go upstairs and go into that room and lock the door. You do trust me don't you?"

Jane nodded and said, "More than anyone."

"Then let's get out and go upstairs casually." Jane nodded as sherry pulled the door handle.

Once they were inside and the door was locked, Sherry asked Jane to sit. Sherry could sense her nervousness as she sat on the bed. Her eyes were widened and she could feel her trembling as she sat next to her.

"Jane I haven't been completely honest with you. Do you remember when you told me that sometimes you don't feel like yourself?" Sherry said.

"Yes." Jane nodded.

"That is because sometimes you are not yourself." Sherry sighed, "Right after I met you, something happened. You spoke to me in a different voice. You introduced yourself to me as Tommy Hill. I did some checking and found out the Tommy disappeared 20 years ago and Mrs. Hill is his mother. I did some investigating and discovered that somehow my husband and his family are involved. Mr. Lipton is as well, the man that tried to choke you today."

"I believe you Sherry, I do. That name Tommy Hill has been repeated over and over in my mind. I couldn't understand why it kept coming to my mind. Does this mean I am possessed?" Jane asked with tears in her eyes.

Sherry chuckled at her sincerely and said, "No, not possessed. I think that somehow he couldn't rest until the truth came out. I have yet to understand why he chose you, but neither of us are safe until we figure out what happened. There is a man that tried to investigate this many years ago. I met him the other day and I feel like we can trust him. I don't know if he will help us or not but I am going to call him and tell him everything. He is our only hope."

Sherry grabbed her phone and searched her contacts for unknown then hit call. He answered right away.

"Hello, you know who this is?" Sherry asked.

"Yes." He answered.

"I need to see you in person, will you come to me?"

"Text the address and then I will delete it."

"Okay." Sherry sent the message and then waited.

There was a knock on the door at 1 o'clock in the morning. Sherry quickly peeped out to find David Keller wearing a baseball cap pulled low to hide his eyes. She opened the door quickly and directed him inside. He noted Jane right away and glanced back at her confused.

"I can explain." Sherry said.

He seated himself at the small table under the lamp and said, "This better be good."

"I haven't told you the truth about everything." Sherry started to explain.

"I don't recall you telling me anything." David said.

"This girl is Jane, Jane Smith. She was given that name because no one knew who she was when she arrived at the hospital with amnesia. I took care of her when she came in through the emergency room having seizures. Shortly afterward, I began visiting her. She sometimes would speak with me in another voice. She would come to me as Tommy Hill. She didn't know and I just told her about it tonight. I paid a visit to Mr. Lipton in the nursing home and he tried to kill her today. I suspect that they know she is tied into this. Now they want her dead."

"You expect me to believe that Tommy Hill has taken over this girl's body and speaks to you?" David chuckled.

"I know how crazy that sounds. This is exactly why I didn't tell anyone about it."

He shook his head and got up to walk toward the door. He stopped as he glanced back toward Sherry and said, "This is a joke. My father was murdered because he wanted to know the truth. You call me here in the middle of the night to play a joke on me?"

"Please, I know it sounds crazy but it is the truth." Sherry shook her head.

He reached for the door knob when suddenly Jane said, "Tommy Hill doesn't lie." In her deep man voice with childish nature.

He stopped and looked back to see her eyes glazed in a trance. He glared toward Jane and said, "Tommy, how old are you?"

"17. Tommy is 17." Tommy replied.

"Tommy, where are you?" David asked.

"I don't know, but it is dark most of the time."

"Tommy, do you know who I am?"

"Yes, I know you. You're David Keller. You go to school with me and you're nice. You gave me your cake once."

David sat down and shook his head and said, "Tommy do you know what happened?"

"I don't remember what happened. I miss Jake and Stephanie. Where did they go? Tommy is all by himself now and doesn't like to be by himself. Where is my momma?"

"I am going to try and figure all this out Tommy, but I need you to be patient. Can you do that Tommy? Can you be patient?" David said.

"Momma said Tommy doesn't have any patience, but I will try."

David replied, "That's good Tommy. You try to be patient."

Jane fell forward as Sherry caught her and helped her to the bed. Sherry covered her with a blanket and laid Jane's head on the pillow. Jane was resting in the bed as David sat back down at the table under the lamp.

"Do you believe me now?" Sherry asked.

He nodded his head and said, "I wouldn't if I hadn't seen it with my own two eyes."

"Please, we need your help."

"I told myself a long time ago that I wouldn't get involved with this again. The truth is, I cannot let it go either. What do you need me to do?"

"I need a place to take Jane that is safe. They are after her now because they know that she has something to do with it." With pleading eyes, she said, "Please, you must know of some place we can take her?"

He hung his head for several seconds then said, "I have a small cabin up by the mountains. Not many know that it is there and even less know that it is mine. I hunt there on occasion. You can both stay there for the time being."

He pulled a pen from his pocket and was drawing on the back of a card from his wallet as he said, "Listen to me, it's imperative that you tell no one of this place. Not even your closest family member. Do you understand me?"

"Yes, tell no one." Sherry nodded.

"I will bring you some food and such tomorrow evening. The two of you must leave before daylight."

"Okay. I will wake her and leave shortly."

"I have a friend that is unemployed right now. I will offer him to come stay with Jane for a small payment. He is a big guy and not afraid of much. I believe he will agree to it. I will call you once I speak with him." David offered.

"Thank you, thank you so much."

He glared at her and said, "This time I am going to see it through. I need to know that you are as well."

"I couldn't walk away even if I tried."

"I will meet you this evening at the cabin."

"I cannot thank you enough."

"Finding out what really happened is enough for me." David nodded.

"We will find out the truth. I promise."

Sherry woke Jane within minutes of David leaving. They gathered their things and were on the road well before daylight. They stopped only for gas and a few snacks. Once they reached the mountain, Sherry pulled over to read the map as Jane slept. She continued to check her rear view to ensure they were not being followed. They arrived at the cabin just before daylight. It was a small cabin with one bedroom. It did have a full kitchen and bathroom. She felt it was perfect for them to hide away in.

They immediately went in and went to sleep. Sherry was exhausted and felt as if it had been days since she had slept. She awoke around noon to find Jane watching television.

"Is everything okay?" Sherry asked.

Jane nodded and said, "I'm just watching cartoons. Is that alright with you?"

"Yes, Jane you can watch cartoons whenever you want." Sherry smiled.

Jane smiled and said, "Good, because I like cartoons."

Sherry sat down beside her and said, "Jane, I want to ask you something but I don't want to offend you."

"It's okay, ask away."

"Okay, I was wondering if you know how to read?"

Jane stopped looking at the television and looked toward Sherry. She lowered her head and said, "I don't know how to read. I guess I was too stupid to learn. I don't know."

Sherry smiled at her and said, "No, maybe no one ever taught you."

"Maybe." Jane shrugged her shoulders.

"How about when all of this is over, I teach you. Would you like that?"

"Yes, I would like that." Jane smiled.

They spent most of the afternoon watching cartoons together. Sherry wondered about Jane as she watched her demeanor and mannerisms. Which appeared to be of a young child of the age 10 or so. She knew the moment that she met her that she felt the need to protect her. Perhaps it was because she was so childlike. She didn't appear to understand the danger of our situation and put all her trust in Sherry. She didn't ever have an opinion or input on our situation either. Sherry felt that she was mentally a young child. Her innocence was astounding as she giggled and watched cartoons. In many ways, Sherry envied her.

David arrived shortly after dark. He brought bags of groceries and cleaning supplies. He was unloading the bags from the trunk as Sherry helped.

"My friend has taken me up on the offer. He will be here shortly. He will be driving a blue car that is older than yours. From here on out, you need to drive it and hide yours behind the cabin." David said.

"Okay."

He grabbed her hand as she reached to grab another bag and said, "Everyone knows your car by now and they will be watching for it."

Sherry nodded and said, "Okay, you're right. I will hide it as soon as we are finished here."

David's friend "Doug" arrived within an hour. He was a tall man that weighed well over 300 pounds. His size was quite intimidating. He had a baby face and immediately took to

Jane. Apparently, he enjoyed cartoons as well. As Jane and Doug watched television, David and Sherry went out onto the porch to talk.

"Doug is a really nice guy. He got hooked up with the wrong crowd and almost got into trouble. I helped him get out of it so, he owes me one. He hasn't been able to secure employment since. I offered him to come here for a small payment. His appearance might seem intimidating, but trust me, he is a big teddy bear." David said.

"I am glad he looks intimidating." Sherry smiled.

"What is our next move?" David asked.

"Ours?" Sherry raised her eyebrows.

"I asked my partners to have a few weeks off. They were kind enough to oblige. I feel like it is unfair for you to go it alone on this. I want to help."

"What is it that you do for a living?" Sherry asked.

"I am an attorney."

"Okay, I feel like we need to go pay Jake a visit. Maybe he remembers something that can help us."

"Let's leave first thing in the morning." David nodded.

The couch let out to a full size bed that Jane and Sherry slept in. David slept in the bedroom and Doug made a pallet on the floor with an air mattress that David had stored at the cabin. Sherry had awoken early and quickly showered then went out on the porch with a cup of coffee. The scenery was breathtaking. It didn't seem as hot on the mountain and there was a breeze that felt almost cool. The mountain seemed tall, it was as if it had risen overnight to hide and protect them from the evil that lurked. There were cactus in every direction that could have been soldiers prepared to battle against anyone attempting to cross into their sanctuary.

Sherry was outside for no more than 30 minutes when David joined her.

"Are you ready?" He asked.

She nodded and said, "Whenever you are."

They were gone after only a quick instruction given to Doug. Tucson was two hours away and they were anxious to speak with Jake. They arrived at the prison shortly before 9 o'clock. They were directed into a small room and made to await Jakes arrival behind the glass window.

Jake arrived with his feet and arms in chains. He was short with red hair and a stocky build. Time had not served him well as he appeared much older than 37. He moved slowly and seemed uninterested in whomever was visiting. He sat down and glared at Sherry through the glass with his slate blue eyes that were hidden behind the wrinkles. She picked up the receiver and placed it to her ear as she watched him do the same.

"Who the fuck are you?" Jake said.

"Sherry Masters."

"You must have married that dick, Joe."

"Yes, I did. But that is not why I am here."

"What the fuck do you want?" Jake asked.

"Look, we only have a short time to talk. It's not enough time for me to explain everything. I came here because I am trying to find out what really happened. I am trying to bring some closure to your mother. I came here because I want you to tell me everything you can about what happened. Anything that might help."

"Do you really think that you can fix this and not get yourself killed in the process? You are a stupid bitch if you do. The cops have it all sewed up and it's been 20 years. I tried to fight it at first. I thought that justice would prevail. Isn't that what they say? Justice will prevail? Well you know what I say now? There isn't no fucking justice. There is the rich and there is the poor. The rich are getting richer and the poor are getting fucked. That's it plain and simple." He leaned in towards the glass and placed his hand open on the glass. He stared at Sherry with sheepish eyes and continued, "These mother fuckers mean business. They will kill you just like they did my brother and Stephanie. The truth is, they will frame someone just like me and he will spend his life in prison for a murder he didn't commit as well. Now do yourself and your family a favor and get in your car and go home. Pretend this never happened and move on."

"I can't." Sherry shook her head.

"Yes, you can." Jake smirked.

"No, I can't. I owe it to your mother, I owe it to Jane and I owe it to David to find out what happened."

Jake looked behind Sherry and noted David at the chair.

"David Keller. I remember his father being killed for doing exactly what you are doing." Jake pointed to David.

"We all need the truth. If we don't find the truth, we cannot heal." Sherry proclaimed.

"It will be hard to heal when you are six feet under."

"It's my decision and I will not stop whether you help me or not."

He leaned back in his chair and looked at her with scolding eyes. "What is it that you want from me?"

"I want to start with the night that Stephanie was murdered."

He nodded his head and said, "Okay." He sighed, "That day had been busy. I had to rush around all day. Lynn had just told me she was pregnant. I was in a state of shock for most of the day. Tommy was excited because there was a school dance that night. It was going to be his first dance with a date. Stephanie was going with him. He loved Stephanie and I loved her too. She was like a little sister to me. Momma had spent the better part of the day making Stephanie a dress to wear. I'll never forget how excited she was when she tried it on." He fought back tears and paused. Once he gained his composure, he continued to explain.

"Tommy had picked out his best suit for the dance. He danced into the room and asked my opinion. I called Lynn and told her that I was going to drop Tommy and Stephanie off at the dance and then would be right over to get her. I drove them to the school then left them there. I went back to get Lynn and she wasn't home. I didn't understand since she didn't seem mad over the phone. I waited for a while and she never showed.

I drove to the store and got a six pack. I parked in the lot across from the school yard and listened to the music coming from the dance and waited for Tommy and Stephanie. Tommy came around 10 and said that Stephanie had gotten a ride with someone else. We drove home and went to bed. Tommy seemed upset on the way home and told me that she had been dancing with your husband and his friends a good part of the night. He said that she refused to leave with him and said that they were taking her home."

"Did Tommy call Stephanie the next day?" Sherry asked.

He shook his head and said, "No, he got his feelings hurt. She was supposed to be his date. He never called to check on her. Several days later, the police barged into our house and arrested me." He looked straight into her eyes and said, "I didn't kill Stephanie. They know I didn't kill her, but they used me as a cover up for whoever did."

"Did you and Lynn talk the next day?"

"She said that she needed time to think. I thought that was odd since she knew I was coming to get her as soon as I dropped Tommy and Stephanie off at the dance."

"What about your best friend Walter? Where was he that night?"

He looked at her sincerely and said, "Walter didn't feel good that night. He had been sick for a couple of days. He wasn't going to the dance or anywhere that night. He was at home."

"Okay."

"The only thing that bothered me about Walter was when we went to court, Walter was subpoenaed and testified as a hostile witness. He told the truth mostly but it hurt. He testified that I would often get drunk and forget what I did. I never forgot anything I did when I was drinking and he knew that. He hasn't visited and I even wrote to him several times. He never answered. We were like brothers."

"If it makes you feel any better, he does visit your mother. He checks on her regularly. She said he brings her food as well."

He leaned back and nodded with a slight smile and said, "Momma loved him almost as much as she loved us. I hope he doesn't believe that I killed Steph."

"I'm guessing if he knew you as well as you say he did, then he knows the truth."

"I hope so." Jake said.

Sherry left there wondering if Jake was a really good con-artist or if he was really framed.

"What do you think?" David asked.

She shrugged her shoulders and said, "I don't know. A part of me wants to believe Jake. The more sensible side of me doesn't know what to believe. I couldn't imagine the anger you would have if you spent 20 years in prison for a murder you didn't commit."

"I knew Jake and he was a drinker. He was trouble all through school but he was loyal to his family. I think Stephanie was like family to him. I always questioned his conviction. I never particularly cared for the guy, but I still never thought he killed that girl."

"What about Walter? Did you know him?"

David nodded and said, "Yes, he was a lot like Jake. They were thicker than thieves. They got arrested several times together as I recall. They were always minor charges like vandalism and public intoxication. You know, petty crimes."

"If they were that close, why didn't Walter ever visit Jake or at least answer his letters?"

"That's a good question. I say we should pay this guy a visit." David suggested.

She nodded and said, "I think we should."

They arrived back at the cabin to find Jane and Doug playing cards. They seemed to be enjoying themselves.

"Who is winning?" Sherry asked.

Doug quickly replied, "Jane is winning. She plays a tough game of Old Maid." Jane laughed.

"I've got steaks to barbecue for tonight. Who's hungry?" David asked.

"Me! I'm hungry." Jane said.

Sherry laughed and said, "I am going to clean the dishes that you two dirtied today first." She was cleaning the kitchen and David was getting the grill ready when her phone rang.

"Hello." Sherry answered the call.

The woman on the other line said, "Yes, This is Lynn Redding. I used to be Lynn Brooks."

"Lynn, I am so glad that you called." Sherry said.

"My mother said that you came by and wanted to speak with me regarding Jake. Listen, I was a different person back then. I don't want to be involved in whatever it is that you are trying to dig up. I've got a husband and children and I have tried to put all of that behind me. I'm sorry that I can't help you."

"I understand but please give me one minute to explain." Sherry pleaded.

"I can't discuss this right now." Lynn said.

"Will you please meet me somewhere? I promise I will not get you involved in anything that anyone will find out about."

Lynn sighed then said, "Meet me at the Dairy Queen on Bridge Street in Chandler at four tomorrow in the afternoon. I will not have long to talk with you. I am picking my child up around there and can only stay a few minutes."

"That sounds great. I will be wearing a blue T-shirt and white shorts."

"Okay. I will find you."

Sherry went back into the kitchen.

"Is everything okay?" David asked.

"Yes, that was Lynn on the phone. Lynn Brooks, Jake's old girlfriend. She has agreed to meet me with me tomorrow in Chandler. Would you like to ride along?" Sherry said.

"I would love to." David nodded.

Chandler was a short drive from Phoenix. They waited until close to one to leave. Sherry could tell by the tone in Lynn's voice that she was not anxious to help. She felt that she needed to be careful in the questions or else she would shut down completely.

They arrived at 3:45 and Sherry got out of the car and went to sit in at the covered area in the front with tables and booths. She had bought a cool drink to sip on since the heat was excruciating that afternoon. She watched as cars came and left and was beginning to think that Lynn wasn't going to show.

Shortly after four, a woman with shoulder length black hair and pale skin approached her.

"Are you Sherry?" Lynn asked.

Sherry smiled and said, "Yes, Please sit."

Lynn sat down and said, "I was reluctant to come. This is dangerous for both of us."

"I've figured that out." Sherry nodded.

"Times were different back then. People were different. I was young and in love and didn't know that sometimes you have to accept defeat and walk away."

"I understand that you have a life and have moved on. What I cannot understand is how so many people can walk away from something like this and not look back. People still suffer for whatever happened back then. Mrs. Hill sits on her porch and cries every day for what she has lost." Sherry said.

Lynn fought back tears and said, "Mrs. Hill and I might not have ever seen eye to eye, but that still doesn't mean that I didn't hurt."

Sherry nodded and said, "What happened to you that night of the dance? The night that Stephanie was killed?"

Lynn leaned back against the metal chair and sipped her drink. She looked at Sherry with shameful eyes and said, "Earlier that day, I had broken the news to Jake that I was pregnant. He seemed excited and was talking about marriage and raising the child. I wasn't ready for that, I was a different person back then. I wanted to do things and raising a child wasn't one of them." She shook her head as she fought back tears. "I loved Jake but we were young. We didn't have money or a means to do that."

"Did you tell him that?" Sherry asked.

Lynn shook her head and said, "No, I wanted to but he was so excited."

"So, what happened?"

"He dropped me off at my house and we made plans to meet that night after he dropped Tommy and Steph at the dance. When he came, I wasn't there. My brother said that he sat outside and honked a few times then left. I confided my situation to my mother and she convinced me to pack my things and go to my fathers in Tucson that night. She drove me down there."

"Why so sudden? I mean, why did she want you to leave that night?" Sherry asked.

"My mother couldn't stand Jake. She never thought he would amount to anything. She was devastated when I told her I was pregnant. She was always threatening to send me to my fathers but that time she meant it."

"It's none of my business, but I have to ask what happened with the pregnancy?"

"My father is a devout catholic and couldn't stand for an abortion. The child was taken the moment that I had it. I have no idea what happened to her."

"When did you move back here?"

"My father moved us back here before I had the baby. His job transferred us. He insisted we live on the opposite side of town as my mother. I've not spoken to anyone from back then since that night. I've wanted to stop by Mrs. Hill's house a million times. I just don't know what to say to her." Lynn had tears in her eyes.

"Did you know Joe Masters?" Sherry asked.

"Yes, He was a total dick. He and his friends were the bullies. They picked on people, made fun of people and were brutally cruel. I hated them and so did Jake."

"Did they pick on Tommy and Stephanie?"

"They picked on everyone that wasn't a part of their group of shit heads. I do recall one time that Joe and his best friend Eric had pinned Tommy up against the lockers and were making him eat some worms that they had dug out of the yard. Tommy was crying as they tortured him. Jake walked up and seen what was going on and beat the shit out of Eric and Joe in front of everyone. They swore to get even."

"Why didn't the school stop this kind of thing?" Sherry asked.

"They didn't stop it because it was the teacher's children doing it. Joe and Eric's mothers were both teachers."

"I have met Eric several times and he always seemed like a nice guy. I guess you never know." Sherry shook her head.

"People change and maybe he did too, I know I have." Lynn sighed.

"Is there anything else you can tell me about that night?"

"Eric and Joe both work for the police department now. When that happened, Eric's dad was the police chief. There was no way anyone could have stepped in and fought the case." Lynn stared into Sherry's eyes and said, "I know Jake didn't kill that girl. I never understood why they framed Jake for it either. When Tommy disappeared, I wondered if he didn't kill himself. He had lost his brother and best friend in a matter of a few days."

Sherry left there feeling as if she never knew her own husband. He was nothing as Lynn had described. She recalled several times that Joe had invited Eric and his wife over for dinner. They had two small children and seemed to be the perfect family. She fought back tears as she wondered how many families might be destroyed over the truth if it is ever revealed.

As they were driving back to the cabin, Sherry asked David to pull over. They stopped and he turned to look at her. She turned to him and said, "I am going to ask you something and I want you to tell me the truth."

He nodded and said, "Okay, I have nothing to hide."

"Was my husband a bully?"

He looked forward toward the mountain that sat in front of them then sighed and said, "Are you sure you want the truth?"

She nodded as she fought back tears.

"Your husband was a total asshole. He had certain people that he allowed in his group and everyone else was shit. He bullied, beat and tortured kids almost daily."

She felt sick and had to throw up several times on the side of the road. Afterward, she was embarrassed as they proceeded back to the cabin. Once they arrived, she sat down to try and collect her thoughts when she heard singing come from the front porch. She quickly realized it was Jane and walked toward the porch.

She found Jane on the porch playing with a jump rope and singing, "Danny, Danny was a big old boy. He needed a bra he could not afford. So all day long we laughed along and sang this little song. Danny, Danny was a big old boy."

"Jane, what are you doing?" Sherry yelled out.

Jane stopped jumping rope and said, "I'm singing."

"Where did you hear that song?"

"I don't know. It was in my head. I hear it over and over in my head." Jane shrugged her shoulders.

Sherry began to cry. She felt horrible for yelling at Jane and ran to her. She hugged her and said, "Jane, I'm sorry. I didn't mean to yell at you. It's not a nice song. Will you please not sing it anymore? Please? Will you do that for me?"

"I'm sorry. I won't sing it anymore." Jane said.

"Thank you."

Sherry wanted to lie down and take a nap. Due to their living situation, she didn't even have a bed to go to. She went back into the living room and sat down where David was watching television.

"What do we do next?" David asked.

"I want to talk to Stephanie's mother. I feel as if I should go alone to do that. I think she might be more receptive to one person." Sherry said.

"I agree. I feel like right now they are not too aware that we are still poking around. They may even think that you left town."

Sherry smiled and said, "I hope so."

Sherry knew that Katherine Masters lived somewhere near the Lipton's. She had no idea exactly where. She decided to have David call as an attorney and speak with Joe's parents to try and find something out about her.

He had his phone set to speaker phone and dialed the number. It rang twice when Joe's mother answered, "Hello." Joe's mother answered.

"Hello, Mrs. Masters?" David asked.

"Yes, may I help you?"

"This is John Douglas. I am an attorney in Phoenix Arizona. I am trying to locate Mrs. Katherine Masters. There is a settlement awaiting her for an old inheritance and I cannot seem to locate her."

"I haven't heard from her in several years. She is my husband's sister and they were never close. If you don't mind holding for a couple of minutes, I can give you the last known address that I had for her."

"No, I don't mind at all." David replied.

After several minutes of both David and Sherry holding their breath that she wouldn't change her mind, she came back on the line and said, "Hello?"

"Yes, ma'am I am still here."

"This is the last known address that I had for her. I have no idea if she is still there."

"Yes, ma'am I understand." David said.

"1423 E. Tucker Drive Phoenix, Arizona."

"Thank you and you have a lovely day." David said before he ended the call.

Sherry used Google Maps and determined the location to be on a very bad side of town. Sherry had never been there due to drive by shootings, robberies and murders. David assured her that she would be safe since he has represented many of them in court. He insisted to go along with her.

They left early the next morning in an attempt to find Katherine. Sherry was nervous most of the drive despite David constantly reassuring her that they would be fine.

"I'm sorry but I have to ask you a question." David said.

"Okay."

"About Jane. I noticed that she seems underdeveloped for her age? I mean, she seems a little slow or struggle with a learning disability?"

Sherry nodded her head and said, "I have wondered the same thing. She doesn't seem to be mentally developed. I am assuming she was born that way."

"My question is this. What happens to Jane when all of this over? Have you thought about that?" David looked over at Sherry.

"I love Jane. She means the world to me. She needs a place to belong. We all need a place to belong. She belongs with me."

He nodded and said, "That is a huge responsibility."

"She belongs with me."

"Okay."

Chapter 4

The drive was long and uncomfortable after their conversation. They entered into the side of town that Katherine lived on to find broken down cars and houses. Many of the houses didn't even appear to be habitable. David drove straight to the address with the help of his GPS. They arrived to find a small child outside playing with a teenage girl in the front yard. The swing set was broken and bent that the child played on. The front porch seemed to be detached from the house. The paint on the house had been worn and chipped over the years to expose only the tattered wood that tried to hold steady despite its age.

The teenage girl was dressed in a pair of cut-off jean shorts and a shirt that appeared too small. She was barefoot and walked slowly on her tiptoes toward the car. The sand was hot and appeared to burn her feet with each step she took. Once she reached the car, she bounced from one foot to the other as her feet sizzled on the street. She couldn't have been over 15 years old. She still donned the acne from the combination of puberty and poor diet. Her hair was short and cut in a pixie which seemed to accentuate her five ear piercings. She spoke with a lisp that was possibly due to the tongue ring which donned a huge white ball.

Sherry rolled down the window and said, "Hello, we are looking for Katherine Masters."

"That's my momma. She isn't here right now. Whatcha want her for?"

"She is not in trouble we are wanting to talk to her about something. What time will she be home?" Sherry replied.

"She was supposed to be home now. I reckon she went by the store or something." The girl shrugged her shoulders.

"Do you mind if we sit here and wait?" Sherry asked.

"I don't care, I reckon that's up to you."

They waited in the car for Katherine. They watched as the young girl played with the small child that couldn't have been over two years old. She played with the child as if it were her baby doll. The baby had a contagious laugh. As they listened to it laugh, they couldn't help but smile each time. The baby was dirty and only had its diaper on. She would swing it around in circles by its arms and it would laugh so hard it would almost choke.

30 minutes after they waited, a woman carrying a brown bag of groceries appeared. She was wearing a waitress outfit that was faded and worn. Her hair was in a bun on top of her head and her shoes were worn canvas slip-ons with holes. She walked slow and leaned forward as if her back had been worn through the years.

As she approached the front yard, the young girl ran to her. She spoke to her as she pointed to David's car parked along the street. The woman gave a confused look as she turned. Sherry stepped out of the car and walked toward her smiling. The woman motioned for the girl to take the baby inside and walked toward Sherry.

"Good afternoon." Sherry smiled.

Katherine nodded and said, "What is it that you want?"

"I don't want anything other than to talk to you."

"Who are you?" Katherine asked.

"My name is Sherry, Sherry Masters."

Katherine stepped back with an appalled look and said, "I don't have anything to say to you."

"Please, wait a minute and let me explain."

Katherine looked at her and said, "Explain what?"

"I am not here on behalf of the Masters. I married a Masters that is the only reason I have that name. I am no longer with him. Joe Masters was my husband." Sherry said.

"You married that little spoiled prick. I guess you figured out what he is really like after you married him?"

"Yes, yes I did."

"What is it that you want from me?"

"I want to talk about Stephanie. I want to find out what really happened to her. No one wants to talk about it. It's important to me that I find the truth."

Katherine looked down and said, "There isn't really anything to tell now. It's so long ago. Why do you care about what happened to her?"

"Because I know that the truth wasn't told. Because people deserve to know the truth."

Katherine motioned to David to come out of the car and said, "Please come in."

Sherry followed her toward the house and looked back to ensure that David followed. They went into a small living room with an old yellow couch that had a daisy pattern. The chair in the corner matched. There was an old braided rug in the center of the floor that was stained and torn. The old box television sitting on the end table appeared to only have reception on occasion.

The teenage girl came out of the bedroom and said, "Mom is there something going on?"

"No dear, they are here to talk about your sister Stephanie." Katherine replied.

The girl's eyes lit up and she said, "Did you know her?"

"No, I'm sorry but I didn't. I do wish I could have." Sherry said.

David chimed in and said, "I knew her. She was one of the most beautiful girls that I have ever met. She was always nice to everyone. She loved to play jokes on people too. I remember one time she put a fake snake in my locker. Then she hid around the corner with a smile from ear to ear waiting on my reaction when I found it."

The girl laughed and said, "I wish I could have known her."

"This is my daughter Trenna, she is 17 years old and I guess you noticed her little one." Katherine pointed toward the baby and said, "That is my grandson Stephen. He is two years old this month."

"Katherine, I called and got your address from your brother's wife. She said that you rarely speak with her or your brother?" David said.

"I cannot pretend that nothing ever happened. I would rather live a happy life with nothing then pretend that everything was okay." Katherine nodded.

"What do you mean?" Sherry asked.

"When Stephanie was killed, they didn't even investigate it. There were so many unanswered questions and no one cared." She looked down and continued, "To begin with, they said that Bill killed himself and I never believed that. He was investigating the death of his own daughter because no one else would. It was obvious to Bill that the department wanted him to let it go. He couldn't. He loved her more than he loved anything or anyone in this world. Bill and I might not have seen eye to eye on much, but we both loved Stephanie wholeheartedly."

They could see that this was not easy for her to talk about. She was fighting back tears as she spoke.

"Did anyone ever make threats to Stephanie? Did you or Bill have and enemies that would want to try and hurt her?" Sherry asked.

"Everyone that met Stephanie loved her. She was a joy to be around. Bill was very well respected and treated everyone with respect. I never had any enemies either that I know of."

Katherine looked toward Stephanie's picture on the wall and then looked down. She looked at Sherry and said, "I will be the first to admit that I wasn't the best mother. I drank daily and partied late most nights. She was a daddy's girl and stayed with Bill more than she ever did with me. I did love her wholeheartedly. I was young and stupid. My biggest regret to this day is that I wasn't the mother that I should have been for Stephanie."

"Besides Tommy, did Stephanie have any other friends or acquaintances she regularly visited?" Sherry asked.

"There were several other children that they played with. Jake had a good friend. His name was Walter and he had a younger sister that would play with them when no one was watching. She didn't like her real friends to see her play with them, though. When she was bored and had nothing else to do, she would play with them. Then when she was at school she would act like she didn't know them."

"What is her name?" Sherry asked.

"Brittney. She was a couple of years younger than Walter. I never heard what happened to her. She didn't show at Stephanie's funeral."

"Thank you for visiting with us. I am going to leave you my phone number and if anything else comes to mind, please call me." Sherry said. Katherine stood up and hugged Sherry.

"I appreciate your effort, but I also fear for your safety." Katherine looked down with a tear in her eye and said, "Sometimes we have to accept things the way that they are."

"Sometimes we can't." Sherry said.

As they drove away, Sherry couldn't help but fight back tears. She imagined the pain she had endured and the struggle she still endures every day.

David looked at her and said, "I think it is time for us to pay Walter a visit."

She nodded and said, "I agree."

They had gone a few miles when Sherry's phone rang. She didn't recognize the number and was hesitant to answer it. She looked at David and he nodded. "Hello." Sherry answered the call.

The woman said, "This is Katherine. I am sorry to bother you. You probably haven't even made it around the block yet."

"No that's fine."

"There is one more thing that I didn't mention."

"What is it?" Sherry asked.

"The locket. Her father gave her his mother's locket. He gave it to her for her birthday when she was 12. She never went anywhere without that locket. She wore it around her neck even when she showered. Her father had put a picture of him on one side and her on the other inside of it. When they found her, she didn't have it on. Bill said that she was wearing it that night when she left. He was very upset about her locket disappearing."

"Thank you. Can you describe the locket to me?"

"It was a bigger than a usual locket. Gold, I am sure real gold. It had a cameo on the front that was pink with a white face."

"Thank you so much for the information. I appreciate it." Sherry ended the call.

"David she was wearing a locket and it disappeared off her body the night she was murdered." Sherry said.

"What kind of locket?" David asked.

"One that she wore every day."

He shrugged his shoulders and said, "Why would anyone want her locket?"

"I have no idea, but I think I may have it." Sherry said.

He immediately pulled the car over and said, "What do you mean you may have it?"

"When Joe and I got married, he gave me a locket as a gift. It's an old locket and fits the description she gave of Stephanie's locket."

"Do you still have it?" He asked.

"I do, it's in my bag at the cabin."

They drove for over an hour to arrive at Reins auto repair. They were greeted by a mechanic at the front of the shop. He was very heavy and short and he had a dip of tobacco in his lip, he spit as they approached him.

"How can I help you?" He said as he wiped the grease off his hands with a towel.

"I would like to speak with Walter Jones." Sherry said.

"Walter?" He asked.

Sherry nodded.

"He is off today and won't be back until the day after tomorrow."

"Okay. It was kind of urgent. Do you know where he lives?"

He shook his head and said, "Now I don't give any information out like that."

"I understand. I'll come back then."

She turned to walk away and he said, "You know what? You seem like a fine young lady. The kind of lady that would enjoy buying lunch for some hungry mechanics. If those mechanics were to accidentally give you an address that is?"

She turned and said, "Will 20 do?"

"30 would."

She handed him 30 dollars and he went inside. She waited for a few minutes and he came back out and handed her a small piece of paper.

She opened it and it read:

2014 Old Union Town Road.

She quickly entered the address in the GPS and they were on their way. It appeared to be a half hour drive. They arrived at an old single wide mobile home. The grass was grown up waist high and windows were broken out and covered in plastic. There were old broken toys laying throughout the yard and the front door was open. The wooden steps were broken in places that led up to the door.

They sat in the car for a moment to check the address when a woman walked out on the porch. She was wearing a yellow pair of sweatpants and a blue tube top. She had her hair up in a bun on top of her head. Her tattoos that sleeved her arms ran up through her shoulder into her neck. She appeared to be in her mid- forties.

Sherry stepped out of the car and said, "Hello."

"Hello, can I help you?" The woman asked.

Sherry said, "We are looking for Walter Jones."

"He is right here." A man suddenly stepped out on the porch. He grabbed the woman's arm and said, "Get your stupid ass back in the house." In a very abrupt manner he pushed her back inside.

David stepped out of the car and said, "Now Walter, we didn't come here to cause any trouble. We just wanted to talk to you that is all."

"Who are you?" Walter asked as he seemed to stagger a bit. He was wearing the same blue mechanics suit that the man had earlier at the shop. An embroidered label on the left side of the chest bore his name.

David walked toward him and said, "Walter, can we talk to you?"

"What is that you want?" Walter said with slurred words.

"We want to talk to you about Stephanie and Tommy." David said.

Walter yelled out, "Get the fuck out of here. Now before I get my gun and pop a cap in your ass." He then yelled, "Connie, get my gun."

They quickly went back toward the car as he said, "You stupid mother fuckers. Do not ever come back here. You hear me! Don't ever come back here."

They quickly sped out of the driveway.

"Why would you act like that unless you have something to hide?" David said.

Sherry nodded and said, "I don't know."

"I think it is time we go to the state police." David said.

"What are we going to tell them?"

"I have a friend that tried to help with this a long time ago. He told me if I ever get more information to let him know."

"Do you have more information?"

"Not really but it cannot hurt to try. I will call him when we get back to the cabin."

They were only about 30 minutes from the cabin when Sherry's phone rang. Joe's name appeared on the caller ID. She turned to David and he nodded for her to answer.

She placed it on speaker phone and said, "Hello."

"You are a stupid bitch. I told you to stop what you are doing, but you refuse to listen. The authorities have been notified of you skipping out with Jane. She was in state custody and you are in trouble. You stupid cunt. You ruined everything. I hope you know that." Joe yelled.

"What are you hiding?" Sherry asked.

"Probably your body pretty soon."

She hung up on him. David pulled over as Sherry fought back tears and said, "I told you this was going to get ugly. This is what they did to me when I tried to investigate this 20 years ago. Think about what you want to do now. We are getting too deep into it and they will come after us."

Sherry nodded and said, "I have to see it through. I already told you." She sobbed, "I have to see it through."

They drove back to the cabin in silence. Sherry had a million thoughts rushing through her mind and she assumed that David did as well. Once they arrived, she felt an urgency to see Jane. She was playing cards with Doug. She seemed oblivious to the problems they faced. She couldn't bear the thought of telling her either.

"Did you see any punch buggies today?" Jane asked.

Sherry asked, "What are punch buggies?"

"You know." Jane said with her hand on her hip.

Sherry nodded and said, "I don't know."

Doug chimed in and said, "That is what we used to call the Volkswagen Beetle. We used to play a game. The game was that if you saw a punch buggy first, you could punch the person next to you."

"Hmmm. I never heard of that." Sherry said.

Jane laughed and said, "You're silly, I thought everyone knew that."

Sherry cooked a small meal and was anxious to retire to bed. She knew she couldn't sleep until everyone else went to bed. She was fighting her exhaustion.

"Can we speak outside for a minute?" David said.

She nodded and followed him out to the patio.

"I called and left a message for my contact. He has retired it seems. I asked if they had anyone that was willing to speak with us. They gave me a new detectives name and number and requested that I contact him. I left him a message on his voicemail. He will not be familiar with the case and that worries me. I expect we will get nothing from this."

"Why can't we catch a break somewhere?" Sherry was tearing up again. "We have to help Jane. She doesn't have anyone else in this world."

"I came into this for my father. I could never rest until I learned the truth about my father. Now I am also in it for Jane. I have grown to care about her as well. That makes me even more determined to learn the truth." David said.

Sherry smiled and said, "Thank you, I appreciate all that you have done, but if you want out then I don't blame you."

"I don't want out. We will do this together. Oh, and by the way if anyone contacts you about Jane's whereabouts then you tell them that she is at Cabana Retirement center in Little Rock Arkansas."

"Okay." Sherry replied, smiling.

"I have a friend that arranged a fake admittance for her there."

"You are one smart cookie." Sherry chuckled.

"I know." David smirked.

Sherry looked around for her bag that she kept the Stephanie's locket in. She was still amazed that it had been Stephanie's this whole time. She took the bag outside and began to search for the locket. She found it and held it up to swing as a pendulum.

"Do you think this could be considered as evidence enough to re-open the case?" Sherry asked.

"No." David shook his head. He looked at her confused and said, "I cannot wrap my brain around why he would give you that locket."

"Maybe since it was a family heirloom he couldn't bear the thought of her being buried in it."

"Maybe or maybe he took it as a trophy and kept it for prestige. You see, the problem is that either way he knows you have it." He sighed and said, "And I bet you that he wants it back."

"I bet you are right."

They walked back into the living room to find Jane and Doug playing cards. Doug had a concerned look on his face and continued to glance toward us. Sherry walked closer to see Jane had an expression on her face that was not normal for her.

"Jane, are you okay?" Sherry asked.

Jane turned toward her and said, "I'm not Jane, I'm Tommy and I am not leaving until somebody finds me."

Sherry turned to David with a frightened look on her face as he walked closer.

"Tommy, why are you doing this to Jane?" David asked.

"Because Jane said that I can. She said that she doesn't mind if I stay for a while." Tommy replied.

Sherry was shaking her head and tearful when David said, "Now Tommy, you know that we are trying to help you."

"But what about Jake? Are you trying to help Jake?" Tommy asked.

"We are trying to help Jake but we don't know if Jake is guilty or not. We are searching for the truth." David answered.

Jane stood up and spread her arm out as she wiped the cards off the table in a fit of rage. She was not even 100 pounds, but seemed to envision her strength of that of 300 pound, six foot tall Tommy. She spoke slowly with a childlike voice of a man as she yelled, "Jake didn't kill nobody. Everybody knows that Jake didn't kill nobody." Then he threw his glass across the room as glass shattered on the wall.

"Tommy, you have got to calm down. We will not help you if you continue to act like this." Sherry demanded.

"Jane said that you are nice people but I don't believe her. You don't seem very nice to me." Tommy said.

"We are nice people but we will not be bullied by you." Sherry said, calmly.

Jane shook her head and sat down. She fell back on the couch as if she were tired.

Sherry grabbed her and asked, "Are you okay?"

She opened her eyes and said, "What happened?"

Sherry smiled and said, "Nothing Jane, nothing."

Sherry felt panicked as it could be only a matter of time before Tommy decides to completely take over Jane's body.

"I think we should take the locket to the state police and turn it in. Maybe it would be enough for them to at least question Joe as to how he got it." David suggested.

"I wonder if he has even thought about the locket. He hasn't asked me about it since I left." She sighed and said, "I am afraid if we do that then he will have even more reason to look for us."

"What do you want to do tomorrow?" David asked.

"I want to find Walter's sister Brittney, if we can." Sherry answered.

He nodded and said, "Okay. One more thing I wanted to ask?"

"Sure, anything."

"Does Joe still go hunting with his buddies all the time?"

"Yes, that used to aggravate me. It seemed every time we had a weekend that we could have spent together, he would say he had a scheduled hunting excursion with his friends."

"Do you know any of their names?"

"A few, why?"

"Nothing, I was just curious."

Sherry couldn't sleep at all. She was thinking about the threat that Tommy had made about taking Jane forever. The next morning David woke her up and went to Sherry.

"What time did you want to leave?" He asked her.

She rubbed her eyes and got up to get dressed. Once she was ready, he asked, "Do we have any idea where we are going?"

"Mrs. Hill was and is still very close to Walter. I suspect she will have some idea about his sister's whereabouts. I think we should pay her a visit because I want to check on her anyway." Sherry suggested.

He nodded and said, "I am ready whenever you are."

They drove to Mrs. Hills and arrived in a little over an hour. She met them on the porch as usual and they were greeted by her huge smile.

Mrs. Hill quickly grabbed them each a huge glasses of tea to take the edge off the Arizona heat and they gathered around the porch. Sherry and Mrs. Hill were barely moving the porch swing that they sat on as David set in the old metal lawn chair across from them.

"How is Jane? Was she not able to come?" Mrs. Hill asked.

"She is fine Mrs. Hill. She was preoccupied but I promise I will bring her soon." Sherry answered.

She nodded and said, "I sure do miss that girl."

"Mrs. Hill, I actually came to ask more questions." Sherry said.

Mrs. Hill looked confused and said, "I believe I have told you everything there is to tell."

Sherry smiled and said, "I know but this is about someone else."

"Okay."

"Do you remember Walter having a sister?"

"Yes, her name was Brittney." She snarled and said, "I never cared for that girl too much. She was the kind of kid that was your friend as long as no one knew it. She would play with Tommy and Stephanie out here at the house, but when they were at school she was mean and cruel." She shook her head and continued, "I guess she got hers in the end."

"What do you mean?" Sherry asked.

"She got on drugs really bad and after several attempts at suicide she eventually lost her mind and started hallucinating dead people were talking to her. She is locked up now at the River Bend Mental Institution."

"How long as she been in there?"

"Oh, a long time. I reckon within a year of Tommy disappearing?"

Sherry turned to David and noted the shock on his face. She wanted to get up and leave right then, but she knew that would be rude since Mrs. Hill wasn't completely aware of why they had been asking so many questions. They finished their tea and were preparing to leave.

"Sherry, I almost forgot to tell you that a man came by here last week looking for you." Mrs. Hill said.

Sherry stopped dead in her tracks and turned to her in shock and said, "Who was it?"

"I believe he said his name was Eric. He said that he was a friend of yours and needed to speak with you. He said that it was urgent."

"What did you tell him?"

"The only thing I knew to tell him. I said I had no idea where you were and hadn't seen you, but the one time you came by a while back." She smiled.

Sherry smiled back and then ran back to the porch to hug her.

They left there, wanting to drive straight to the River Bend Mental Institution but David said that they should go tomorrow since it was getting late. Sherry did feel the need to see Jane's face and make sure she was safe.

They arrived at the cabin around three that afternoon.

"I am going to take a trip into town and grab us some groceries and a few other things that we need." David said.

"I will wait here with Jane and Doug." Sherry smiled, "I can do some much needed cleaning while you are away."

He gave a smirk and said, "That sounds wonderful."

He left at four that afternoon and it was getting dark outside yet, he hadn't returned. Sherry was getting worried by eleven that evening and could tell that Doug was as well.

"Doug, do you think we should go out and look for him?" Sherry asked.

"I don't know. Have you tried calling him?" Doug asked.

"I have and it goes straight to voicemail every time."

"I could go look for him, but I don't want to leave you and Jane alone."

"I could go but I don't want to leave you and Jane alone either."

"Maybe we should all go together?" Doug shrugged his shoulders.

"I agree, we will all go."

She quickly readied Jane and they were in the car within a few minutes.

"Why are we going out so late?" Jane asked.

"We are going to find David." Sherry replied.

"Is he missing?" Jane's eyes grew bigger.

"I hope not but if he is we will find him."

They were in route to Phoenix traveling slowly watching out the windows for his car. The glistening lights of the city could be seen off in the distance resembling that of a silhouette of stars when Sherry noted headlights from behind arriving at an alarming rate. She felt a rush of heat to her head as panic set in. She turned to Doug as his face implied he had noticed the oncoming approach.

"We have to stay focused and calm." Sherry said.

He nodded and said, "Maybe it's just someone in a hurry and they will pass." She was praying he was right.

As the lights grew nearer, they slowed behind them. Then suddenly, police lights gleamed behind them.

"Should we pull over?" Doug asked.

"I don't know what to do." Sherry said.

"I think we should pull over. It's probably an officer from this area and he is wondering where we are going."

He slowed and pulled off the side of the road on the dark desolate highway. There wasn't another vehicle in sight. Sherry felt an overwhelming panic and fear. She knew in her gut that this was a mistake, but had wanted to trust that she was wrong.

Jane sat in the backseat calmly and asked, "What did we do wrong?"

Sherry turned to her and said, "Nothing Jane, they just want to ask what we are doing."

"Why?"

"I don't know but don't worry, everything is fine."

An officer that she didn't recognize approached Doug's window and said, "Good evening."

"Good evening officer." Doug nodded.

"Do you have your license and registration?"

He reached into his pocket and donned his license then pointed to the glove box for the registration. Sherry leaned in and grabbed it then handed it to him.

The officer studied them in his hands momentarily then said, "Do you mind stepping out of the car for a minute?"

"May I ask why?" Doug asked.

The officer reached and pulled the door handle and said, "Sir, I need you to step out of the vehicle."

Doug turned to Sherry with a disheartening look of dismay and he stepped out of the vehicle. He followed the officer to the back of the vehicle as Sherry watched. She could feel her heart pounding and she was struggling to breathe. She could feel the panic sat in as she struggled to clear her mind.

She heard an argument ensued between Doug and the officer. There was a small struggle then a gunshot. Jane screamed as Sherry jumped into the driver's seat and started the car. They were speeding away as the officer was grabbing the driver's door handle. He began firing shots toward the car as Sherry cried out for Jane to lay down in the seat. He was following them with his lights gleaming within seconds. She drove faster than she was comfortable with as he tried several times to pull beside them and force them off the road. She held her ground and pushed back. She called out to Jane, asking if she was alright as her cries of fear from the backseat seemed to echo throughout.

"What is happening?" Jane cried.

The pursuit continued for several miles. They were approaching the edge of Phoenix when she noted the car to disappear from behind them. She was shaken to the point that she couldn't stop trembling. She continued to drive for another hour. She took several turns and made a few circles to ensure that no one was following. She pulled into a 24 hour diner.

"Jane, let's get out and go inside. I want to make a few phone calls." Sherry nodded.

As she turned to Jane, she was wiping her tears.

"What is happening? Is Doug dead?" Jane asked.

"Listen to me Jane. We have to get out of this car and go inside and appear as if we are okay." She nodded.

Once they were inside and seated, she studied the patrons scattered throughout the diner. There were only a few and most appeared to be drunks having coffee after drinking their night away. The waitress was friendly and brought coffee quickly. Sherry was still trembling as she tried to pull her phone from her pocket. She dialed 911 then canceled the call. She studied Jane's face and fear in her eyes. She felt her heart sink.

"Jane, are you hungry?" Sherry asked.

"No."

"I don't know what to do."

Jane wiped her tears that were running down her cheeks.

"It's going to be okay, we will figure it out together." Sherry said as she reached to hold her hand.

She glanced at the time on her phone and it was one in the morning. David had not called and she felt as if he had probably suffered the same fate as Doug. They had nothing with them and couldn't go back to the cabin. They sipped their coffee for over an hour then Sherry decided to drive farther into town and get a motel. They rented a room in the center of Phoenix that seemed off the grid. She parked the car in the very back and they walked to their room. She locked the door using the dead bolt and told Jane that they needed to sleep.

When she awoke she grabbed her phone to check the time and noted a missed call from David. She sat up and immediately called his number back.

"Listen to me, you have got to grab Jane and get the hell out of there." David said.

"Where are you?"

"They got me last night on my way back. They ran me off the road and left me for dead. I woke up in my car upside down off the side of the road. I hitched a ride to town and have spent the night at the hospital."

"Which hospital are you at?"

"They are releasing me right now at Phoenix General."

"We are on our way." She quickly woke Jane and were out the door in minutes.

She arrived to find David sitting in the Lobby with his right arm in a cast. His face was bruised and he appeared battered throughout. He walked slowly as if each step pained him. Once they were in the car, Sherry leaned on the steering wheel and cried.

"What? This isn't anything to cry about. I am fine." David said.

She shook her head and said, "Doug, they killed Doug last night. We went to look for you and thought a police officer was pulling us over, but it was one of them and they shot Doug. I sped away and they followed us until we reached Phoenix."

He sighed and said, "We have to find someone to listen to us."

Sherry nodded in agreeance.

They drove to the state police building and went inside. They asked to speak to an investigator and explained that they had information to give regarding a murder. Within minutes, a young man appearing to be in his mid-twenties came from behind them and guided them into a small office. They told of their incidents from the night before and of the disappearance of Tommy Hill. They suggested that it had something to do with the murder of Stephanie Kramer.

He seemed nice and he showed interest in their stories. Despite his interest, they still left there feeling as if they were alone. They knew that they couldn't go back to the cabin and Sherry suggested to David that they stay night by night at different motels.

"Do you feel like taking a trip to River Bend Mental Health Institution today?" Sherry asked.

He nodded and said, "Why not?"

Sherry googled and found it to be only about an hour drive from the police station. They hurried on their way and were there in less than an hour. It was a large facility that featured several stories and seemed to have an abundance of helpful and friendly staff.

A nice older lady at the desk asked, "Can I help you?" She was wearing a scrubs and appeared to be anxious to help them with a smile.

"Actually we came here to see Brittney Jones." Sherry said.

"Can I ask your name?"

"Sherry Masters.

Inquisitively, the nurse smiled and said, "I am just asking because some of our patients can only have approved visitors and she is one of them.

"What do you mean, approved visitors?"

"They have a list of names and only those may visit. Brittney is one of them."

Sherry turned to David knowing they would not be visiting Brittney. They waited and she was back within minutes to inform them that they were not on the list.

They walked back to their car without any words between them.

"I am so sorry David. I feel like I drug you back into something that is going to get you killed with me and Jane." Sherry said as she buried her face into her hands.

"Listen to me, I came here knowing what I was getting into. I don't blame you or Jane either one. I could never rest not knowing what happened to my father anyway."

"You never really told us the story of your father."

"My father was a state police investigator. When Stephanie was murdered, they wanted my father to investigate the case. He started finding holes in the case against Jake and wanted an investigation against the entire Phoenix Police Department. Within weeks, he was shot by an alleged car thief. I never believed it and neither did his partner. His partner knew things were not right but let it go. He retired a couple of years ago and I haven't spoken to him since my father's funeral."

"Do you think he would talk to us now?"

"I suppose we could try."

He directed Sherry to a small urban community of average houses and they stopped in front of a small house that was painted white and had blue shutters. The yard was perfectly manicured with cactus plants decorating the front.

"This is where he lived last I knew. He and my father were close friends and we used to visit frequently all through my childhood and up until my father was shot. I don't know if he still lives here or not, but we can knock and ask?" David said.

"What is his name?"

"Ray Carter and his wife, Diana Carter. They had a son that was near my age, but he was learning disabled. His name was Brian and they home schooled him. We used to play together whenever we visited. I was only 17 when my father was murdered so after that, we rarely visited." He sighed and continued, "When I was investigating my father's death after I had come back from college, Ray paid me a visit. He told me that I needed to let it go and move on with my life. He begged and said that he didn't want to see my mother bury the only thing she had left." He turned to Sherry and gazed into her eyes and said, "Ray was a good man, but I always felt like he knew more than he was telling."

"Maybe he has had a change of heart now."

He nodded and said, "I guess we are going to find out."

They approached the door and David rang the doorbell. There were two cars in the driveway so they felt confident that someone was at home. The door slowly opened to reveal a woman that appeared to be in her late sixties. She was short and heavy with gray hair that lacked attention. Sherry felt as if they had awoken her. The woman immediately smiled once she seen David and threw the door open to hug him. She seemed excited as she was hugging him and bouncing side to side.

"Now who do we have here?" The woman said, glancing toward Jane and Sherry.

"I'm sorry, this is Jane and this is Sherry. They are friends of mine." David said as he gestured toward them.

"Wonderful, just have a seat anywhere you want. I'll go wake Ray." She left the room giddy and returned a few minutes later announcing he would be right out.

She offered tea and glasses for everyone.

When she returned David asked, "Where is Brian?"

She stopped smiling and looked at David sullenly and said, "I thought you knew David."

"Knew what?" He said.

"Brian was ran over by a car in front of our house five years ago. He was killed instantly."

David looked down as if in complete shock. He shook his head and stood up to hug her. "I am so sorry, I didn't know."

"That's okay David, I suppose we should have called."

Ray appeared from the hallway reaching out for David. David hugged him tightly as if he had reunited with a long lost family member.

"I am so happy that you came by to visit. We have missed seeing you for so long. After Brian was killed, we longed for the company of those who knew him best." Ray said.

David nodded and said, "I'm sorry I haven't visited and Diana just told me of Brian's death."

"I wanted to call you, but I didn't want to make you feel obligated to come. You were busy and besides, there was nothing you could do anyway." Ray said.

"But he was like a brother to me."

"I know, but I didn't want to bring up old feelings for you either."

"What do you mean?" David asked.

"Nothing, I didn't mean nothing."

David turned to Diana and said, "Diana, would you take Jane into the other room and get her snack?"

Diane nodded as she turned to Ray.

Ray nodded and said, "Diana, why don't you let her try some of those cookies you made yesterday." He smiled at Jane and said, "She makes the best cookies around."

"You know something that you are not telling?" David asked.

"You have made a good life for yourself son. You need to take that and move on." Ray shook his head.

"Who ran over Brian?"

"It was a Phoenix police officer. He claimed that Brian ran out in front of his car." Ray answered as he shook his head and looked down.

"You didn't believe that, did you?"

"No, Brian knew how to stay out of the road and watch for cars."

David stood up and said, "Okay Ray, you are like a father to me and it's time to come clean and tell me whatever you know."

"Ray don't do that, please, it might get him killed." Diana pleaded.

Ray turned to her and said, "He will never let it rest anyway."

She turned to hide her tears.

"When your father grew suspicious of the allegations made against Jake not being substantiated, he began to investigate and ask questions. The Phoenix police didn't like state getting involved in their cases and warned him to back off. He told me that he was sure that the kid accused of the crime didn't commit it. He said that threats were made against himself and his family. You are too much like your father because he couldn't let it go either. He learned that other kids with disabilities were going missing as well. It angered him in wondering if they were deliberately hurting people that were less able to defend themselves and perhaps more trusting of the human race.

He began investigating an officer by the name of Martin Masters. He was the captain of the department and your father described him as being a bully. He said that he was in his office and saw his keys laying on his desk. He had a Pez candy dispenser attached to it that fit the description of one that a kid that was murdered was alleged to have had in his possession when he disappeared.

He said when he asked him where he got it, Masters grew defensive and angry. That made him suspicious of the captain and he told me he was going to request more officers join in the investigation. He confided this to me an hour before his death." He sighed and continued, "It seems that many murderers enjoy taking trophies from their victims and your father felt that the Pez candy dispenser was a trophy."

"Do you feel like Brian's death was really intentional?" David asked.

"I don't know if it was or not. I do know that there was certainly some irony in the case. The funny thing is that three days before his death, he told me that a cop came by and asked to see me. He told him I wasn't home but would be back later. He said that the cop seemed anxious and wanted to visit so he let him in. Brian had a pet rock that he carried in his pocket and petted constantly." He sighed and then said, "I feel certain in saying he was petting the rock while the officer was here." He glared into David's eyes as he said, "We buried Brian without his rock. We couldn't find it anywhere and he was never without it in his possession.

About a year before Brian was killed, there was a girl near our neighborhood that disappeared. Brian knew her and used to play with her on occasion. Her mother was rarely home and she had made an agreement with Diana to bring her and leave her on occasion. She was much younger than Brian, but they played games together and watched television. They met at the library and Diana took an immediate liking to her mother. She was a single mother that worked two jobs trying to make ends meet and Brian enjoyed the company.

The girls name was Rebecca and she was here at least twice a week for over three years. One night, her mother woke us late in the evening beating on the door. She was frantic and said that Rebecca had disappeared. We called the police right away but she was never found. I pushed for a state investigation at the office. The city didn't appreciate that very much and I was told to let them handle their investigation and to keep my nose out of it. I didn't push too hard, but I felt as if I might have stepped on some toes. The next thing I knew, Brian was dead in the street and I had nothing left."

Sherry could see the tears welling in his eyes as he excused himself from the room and exited toward the hallway. David appeared to be holding his own tears back.

When Ray retuned after several minutes, he said, "I'm sorry, but this is a very emotional conversation for me." He placed his arm on David's shoulder and said, "David, I have always been a coward. I was a coward when your father was killed. I was a coward when Rebecca disappeared. What's worse is that I was a coward when my own son was murdered. I was a coward because I felt like I had to protect what was mine. I have nothing left to lose, mostly because there is nothing left of the man that I was back then. There is just an empty shell of what used to be."

"I'm sorry that I came and drudged up all of the pain that you had laid to rest." David said.

"David, my pain can never rest. The pain that we have endured is drilled into our very souls. Even in death, this pain will continue. This is the kind of pain that needs to be set free in order to sleep. Vengeance is my key to freedom and I desire it from the depth of my very soul."

"I would like to share our story with you if you have time." David said.

"The only thing I have left in this world is time. Please share your story with me." Ray smiled.

Chapter 5

Once Ray had been enlightened and understood the danger that they were in, he quickly told them of a small trailer he owned near the river and gave them the key. He welcomed them to use it as long as they needed and begged them to keep in touch and advise if they needed anything else.

Sherry left there feeling as if her own family may soon be enduring the same pain that Brian's, Stephanie's, Tommy's, and Rebecca's family were feeling. Somehow, it didn't seem fair when she realized that there wouldn't be anyone to endure the pain of Jane's death once she was gone. It was sobering to realize how lonesome it must feel in realizing that there wasn't anyone out there to miss you. It was surreal to understand that she wouldn't miss what she has never had.

They drove for over an hour watching cautiously in their rear view mirror ensuring that we were not followed. They arrived at a small trailer in the mountains that appeared to have been made in the seventies. Ray said it was his getaway and he used it when he needed to be alone. It had three rooms and a bathroom but two beds and a couch. Perfect for them and Sherry was offered one of the beds. Jane was eager for the couch that was sitting directly in front of the television.

She was so much like a child that it hurt Sherry to know that she couldn't protect her the way she needed. She had no idea they were being tracked by murderers or that she was in grave danger. Somehow, that did make it easier for Sherry in knowing that she didn't have to cope with the fear mechanism of the ordeal.

Sherry couldn't help, but feel they had turned David's entire life upside down. Although she wouldn't have blamed him if he decided to make a run for it, she prayed he wouldn't.

Sherry had locked the door and turned the light off. She was going to lay down for the night when she noted Jane had sat back up on the couch.

"What's wrong Jane? I thought you were tired." Sherry asked Jane.

Jane answered in Tommy's voice, "I didn't mean to get you killed."

"What?" Sherry asked as her face went pale.

"I didn't want to get you killed. I'm sorry." Tommy said.

Sherry walked toward her on the couch and said, "Tommy, you aren't going to get me killed."

"Yes, yes I am. Tommy always does stupid stuff. I know I'm not smart but I like you. I should have never came."

"Tommy, don't blame yourself."

"I wanted to help Jake. I didn't want Jake to die in prison. He loved me and Stephanie and it wasn't fair."

"I know Tommy, I know."

He laid back on the couch sobbing and she watched as he drifted off to sleep.

The next morning David said, "I have thought about it and I have decided that I am going to contact the FBI. Maybe someone there will give a shit about our situation."

"It cannot hurt, can it?" Sherry said.

"I want you and Jane to stay here and I will drive in to the federal building and see if anyone is interested in listening to us."

"Do you think we would be better off sticking together?"

"I will not be gone long, I promise."

Sherry sighed.

He consolingly said, "I feel like you and Jane are safer here. No one knows about this place and if they agree to talk to us then I will come back and we can go together."

"Okay."

Sherry didn't like the idea of separating, but David felt they were safer hiding in the trailer. He left that morning around ten and promised to call once he arrived at the federal building. He had been gone around an hour when he called to tell her that he had made it safely. He said that he was waiting on an agent to speak with him.

Jane and Sherry were playing dominoes, trying to pass the time. Suddenly, there was a rumble outside then the door was kicked in and two large men bolted toward them wearing masks. They tried fighting back but it was futile. They had no warning the men were coming and no weapons to fend them off with.

The men gagged their mouths then placed cotton sacks over their heads. They quickly tied their arms and legs behind them dragging them by the ropes. They patted them down, removing their phones. They were rough and hurried as they threw them into what felt like a car trunk. They were tossed in like sacks of trash and the sound of the door closing echoed into their brain. Sherry knew that Jane was beside her because she could hear her cries. Through all of their wiggling and squirming, they made no progress toward freeing themselves. They drove for what seemed like an eternity as Sherry listened to Janes cries and felt her heartbeat in her throat.

Once Sherry felt that the car had slowed and she could no longer hear the roar of the engine, she felt as if she had met her destiny and prayed it would be quick. The trunk hatch opened and someone grabbed them, dragging them by the ropes around their feet and hands. The pain was excruciating, but Sherry couldn't scream. She could hear Jane whimpering nearby. She was dropped on her face somewhere a few minutes later and heard a door slam.

Sherry felt as if it was becoming difficult to breathe with the sack over her head. She wondered if she would lose consciousness and die from lack of oxygen. She felt panicked and tried to slow her breathing but her thoughts were running ramped. Her heart ached for Jane in realizing that if she had never met her then she wouldn't be here now.

She heard the door open and heavy footsteps marching what seemed closer. Suddenly, her head was jerked about, removing the sack from her head. She opened her eyes to reveal a large man that she didn't recognize with red curly hair and a scruffy beard.

"Well, hello beautiful." The man said.

She turned to see Jane and noted that she also had her sack removed from her head. Her face was red and eyes swollen as tears still dangled from her cheeks.

He removed their gags and using a sharp knife with a quick swipe their feet and hands were free. He walked out quickly as Sherry listened to the lock click on the other side of the door. Jane scooted closer to Sherry as they cuddled in a corner.

"What are they going to do to us?" Jane asked.

"I don't know Jane, but I am so sorry that this happened." Sherry tried to fight back tears in realizing that she needed to be the strong one right now.

Sherry kept telling herself to remain calm, but the panic she was feeling was overwhelming. She knew that no one would have a clue where they were. She felt responsible for Jane and the guilt was causing her heart to ache immensely as she fought the fear that was trying to overtake her.

They could hear several different men's voices outside the door. They could hear laughter and talking, but wasn't able to decipher what they were saying. She tried to concentrate on the voices when she felt Jane begin to jerk in her arms. She turned to see her convulsing with her eyes rolled back and frothy liquid rolling from her mouth.

"Jane! Jane! Oh god no, Please!" Sherry cried out.

The door opened and a large man with brown hair and Scruffy brown beard that she didn't recognize came into the room and said, "Hey, Keep it down here or we will gag you again." He noted she was convulsing and called out, "Fred, you better get in here. The retard is having some kind of seizure or something."

The big man with the red hair came back in and noted Jane still jerking as she convulsed and said, "Well fuck. Now what do we do?" Looking to his partner.

His partner shrugged his shoulders and said, "Aren't you a fucking nurse? Do something you stupid bitch." Pointing to Sherry.

Sherry asked, "Can I please get a pillow and blanket?"

They turned to each other and shrugged their shoulders as one exited the room to fetch them.

They threw the pillow and blanket toward Sherry as they exited the room. Sherry placed her head on the pillow and covered her up as she rolled her on her side. It was all that I could do for her besides praying. After several minutes, Jane stopped jerking and was still breathing. Sherry allowed her to rest.

When she opened her eyes again she wasn't Jane. It was Tommy and he immediately said, "I know this room. I have been here before, I remember." Tommy recalled.

"What do you remember Tommy?" Sherry asked.

"They locked me in here before they hunted me."

"What do you mean before they hunted you?"

"I ran and they found me."

"Where are we Tommy?"

"I don't know. I don't remember. Tommy is stupid and can't remember."

"No, No, Tommy is not stupid. Don't say that."

"I want my momma." Tommy said as he cried.

The door opened again and this time both men entered. The one they called Fred said, "Is the retard okay?"

Sherry didn't answer so he kicked her leg with his large boot and said, "I'm talking to you bitch! I said, is the retard okay?"

Sherry nodded as she held her calf in pain.

The men left the room, again securing the latch on the other side.

Tommy said, "They are really bad men. Tommy knows they are bad men."

"Yes, Tommy they are bad men. What else can you tell me about these men Tommy?"

"They are mean and like to hurt people. They told me if I didn't do whatever they wanted me to do that they were going to hurt my momma."

"I'm sorry Tommy. I wanted to help you, but it seems I have made matters worse."

"I'm sorry that I got you and Jane killed."

When Tommy said those words to her, she felt an absolution take hold of her that brought on a numbness that felt cold and silent. She wasn't sure how to reply, so she didn't. She felt as if those words could very well be the last truth she ever hears. She wasn't sure what torture she was about to endure but knew that she would die with the honor of knowing that she did so in trying to save someone worth saving.

Tommy and Sherry sat in silence for several hours. She wondered how he must have felt in knowing that he was going to die twice by the same hands.

He turned to her and said, "You tried to help Tommy and I like you."

"I like you too Tommy."

"I am going to stay, if you don't mind."

"I would rather you did stay Tommy. It might make it easier for Jane."

It was hot in the small room and they never offered light as the darkness set in around them. Sometime during the night, the door was opened and two men rushed in to grab Sherry. They drug her out kicking and screaming into another room where several men wearing masks took turns raping her. She tried to fight back, but their strength was unimaginable. She was thrown back into the room with Tommy once they were finished. She was so sore and could barely move, the pain was unbearable. She awoke some time later with her head in Tommy's lap and him brushing her hair with his fingers.

"Please don't leave me here by myself. I don't want to die alone again, please." Tommy pleaded.

She turned to roll over on her other side as she cried.

As dawn seemed to be creeping in through their only window, the door opened again. Fred marched in quickly and sat down on a small tray bearing water and two donuts.

He smirked and said, "Eat up darling. You're going to need your strength."

Sherry was so sore she could barely move, every inch of her body ached.

Tommy scooted over and grabbed the one pitcher of water and two donuts then scooted back to her to share.

"Tommy, you eat the donuts. I don't want any."

"Please, you have to eat. I don't want to die alone again."

Sherry slowly eased up and took the donut from his hand and forced herself to eat it. They shared the water in silence awaiting their next round of terror.

"Tommy, I don't want to die here." Sherry cried.

"It's better when it's over because it don't hurt anymore."

Sherry felt as if he were probably right and she didn't want to hurt anymore. She wondered how many of them there were. She knew there had to be at least three or four, but since they had blindfolded her as they raped her, she couldn't be certain.

As darkness fell again, they were beginning to lose track of time. Sherry wasn't even sure what day it was anymore. The amount of water and food they were bringing them wasn't near enough and the room was so hot it was taking its toll on both of them. Sherry felt weak and nauseated most of the time. The door opened and she was blindfolded and drug out again. They repeatedly raped her, beat me and threw her back in the room. She crawled toward Tommy, unable to speak as he placed a pillow under her head and held her. He sobbed as he tried to rock her in his arms.

The next morning, Fred delivered two donuts and a pitcher of water as he had the day before. He kicked Sherry in her side and said, "You better tell the retard to get some exercise because she is going to need it." He slammed the door shut as he laughed.

Sherry tried to force herself to sit up and leaned against the wall. She said, "Tommy, do you know what he meant?"

"I think they are going to do what they did last time to me." Tommy said as he lowered his head.

Sherry said, "What did they do?"

"They let me loose and told me to run if I want to live. I ran as fast as I could but they found me."

"What is the point in that?"

"They call it a big game hunt."

"They hunt people?"

"They hunt people like me and Stephanie."

Sherry cried as she realized that Jane was going to be released into the woods and then hunted by grown men as if she were a deer or bear. She couldn't run very fast due to her leg being turned in. Her tiny body would never survive in the woods alone. She tried to convince herself that Tommy was there and he was going to help her, but she knew that he couldn't survive it either. He was being forced into being hunted again as if he were a big game trophy and he already knew his fate was sealed.

Sherry prayed that they would finish her off first and she wouldn't have to witness Jane's death. She heard the lock being turned on the other side and footsteps entering the room. She was laying with her back to the door. The footsteps drew closer then stopped. She didn't turn to see which of the two bastards had entered. Then she heard Joe's voice.

"Hey baby, are you a little sore?" Joe said.

She cried out, "No, tell me that it's not you."

"Oh, but we were so happy, at least until you fucked it all up."

She couldn't turn to look at him. All of her suspicions were now confirmed. The man that she had loved and married was the one responsible for all of these deaths and even her own very soon.

"Why?" She cried out.

"You are such a stupid little cunt. You couldn't keep your nose out of other people's business and now look at you. You're just a weak little cunt alone on the floor and nobody even misses you."

She raised up on her arms and turned to look him in his eyes and then spit in his face.

He slapped her, he slapped her so hard that she fell to the floor.

She cried out, "I hate you, you bastard."

He laughed so loud it echoed off the walls. She watched his shadow bounce off the wall as he danced his way out of the room.

A part of her had known it was him, but an even bigger part of her didn't want to believe it. She felt as if she was stupid because she should have seen it all along. He was always taking long hunting trips and she had also often heard him refer to people that were mentally or physically challenged as retards or even watched him make fun of them. That had always irritated her but she thought it was probably what he had been taught.

Her lip was bleeding as she tried to pull herself back up to sit against the wall next to Tommy. He was crying in the corner with his hand over his mouth and looking away.

She steadied herself next to him and said, "Listen to me Tommy."

He shook his head and was refusing to turn toward her. She grabbed his chin and pulled it toward her and said, "Please Tommy, I need you to listen to me."

He steadied his eyes on her and she said, "When they turn you loose and start their hunt, I want you to promise me that you will run, run as fast and far as you can and not look back. I want you to make it to a street somewhere and flag down a ride and get out of here."

He nodded his head and said, "I don't know which way to go or how far."

"You just go and keep going until you find someone or a street."

"What about you?"

"Don't worry about me. Please, save Jane. Will you promise me that you will do your best to save Jane?"

"Yes."

Sherry was becoming weaker and wanting to sleep most days. The pain was endless as they continued to rape and beat her nightly. She could sense they were growing bored of her and wondered when the end would finally come. She couldn't stand or walk any longer. She was certain her right arm was fractured. Tommy was having to help her slowly sip water. She had no idea how long they had been there and had accepted the fact that we were not going to be found. She sensed Tommy was much weaker as well and his tiny body wouldn't be able to make it far before the huntsmen found their prey once he was released.

She felt as if all hope had been lost and had come to terms with the fact that Jane and her would both meet their final destiny at this lonely cabin at the hands of these sick bastards. Her heart ached in wondering how many others had already and how many more would meet the same fate here as well.

The darkness fell as she lay there feeling as if she couldn't suffer at their hands one more time. She awaited their arrival as she pondered ideas of how to make them end it for her. She thought to herself, "I could try scratching or biting them?" She must have drifted off because she awoke to daylight and they hadn't come for her.

"Tommy, I think they have grown bored of me now. They didn't come for me." She said.

"Maybe it's my turn to entertain them." He lowered his head.

"That is what I was thinking. Please, remember to run and run and not look back or stop."

"I'll never make it."

"No, don't say that. You can and you will."

He reached out and grabbed her hand and said, "I know you want to believe that, but trust me, I know."

As daylight sat in stronger, they waited for their water. The door opened and Fred brought their water in. This time he brought two pitchers of water and two donuts.

He sat them down and smiled then said, "Enjoy."

Sherry turned to Tommy and Said, "Tommy, drink them both and eat them both."

"No, you have one." Fred said, sternly.

"Listen to me Tommy, you are our only hope and you need your strength. You drink all of the water and eat both donuts. You are going to need the strength to try and get out of here and find help." Sherry pleaded.

"I will not eat or drink unless you do." Tommy shook his head.

"Okay, Ill drink half the pitcher of my water if you will drink the other half, please."

"Okay."

They waited for them to come as dusk began to settle in from the window in the room. Fred came back into the room after darkness had set in.

"What's wrong? Are you growing bored?" Fred smiled.

Sherry stared at him as he continued, "We need a woman to come clean our kitchen for us and Joe said you're a good housekeeper."

Sherry couldn't stand up as he tried to force her up to come with him. Once he had assisted her to stand and noted her weakness, he said, "You worthless bitch." As he threw her back to the wall and she fell to the floor.

Her arm that was fractured ached and throbbed as she tried to steady herself again. Her ribs hurt with every breath she took. Within minutes of Fred leaving the room, Joe came in. He slowly walked toward her holding a pair of pliers in his hand. His footsteps echoed like a tap dancer off the cold tile floor. He knelt down beside Sherry as she gasped for air.

"You really are a pitiful little cunt." Joe said and turned to Tommy with a big smile. "I bet you are a worthless little cunt too, you retard."

Sherry's ribs ached, her arm throbbed and sweat poured from her face as she tried not to vomit.

"Do you know what happens to women when they don't obey their husbands?" Joe asked.

She continued to try to catch her breath.

"Well, they lose a finger." He reached down grabbing her right wrist and pulled it higher. He took the pliers and snipped off half of her pinky finger. It cracked like a Popsicle stick and could be heard and felt throughout the room. Blood spattered on the wall behind her. She was already in so much pain that she didn't feel it. Tommy cried out in fear.

Joe stood up and said, "What's wrong retard? Haven't you ever seen blood before?" Maybe I should cut yours off too."

Tommy silenced himself by putting his hands over his mouth. Joe whistled the tune, "I wish I was in Dixie hooray, hooray." As he tap danced out of the room.

They didn't have anything to control the bleeding and Sherry was too weak to search. She had settled into a numbness that was taking hold and she felt complacent with it. Tommy tore the end of his shirt off and quickly tied it around her amputated finger.

Cold sweat was pouring off her face as she said, "Tommy, don't look back, run and don't look back."

He cried, "I don't want to leave you here."

"Please, save Jane. She needs you." She was so tired and weak, she had nothing left to give.

Sherry passed out. When she awoke, it was breaking dawn through their small window. As daylight settled in, the door opened again. Four men, one being her husband came through the door.

"Okay retard, today is the day. We have to go back to work tomorrow, vacation is over. Time to clean up the mess, Oh, and guess what? You retards are the mess." Joe kicked Sherry and said, "We really just have to bury this one. She is about done for anyway." He laughed and continued, "I guess play time is over for this cunt."

Sherry squeezed Jane's hand and felt her squeeze back. She was too weak to move and they knew it.

Two of them grabbed Jane and led her out of the room. Sherry watched, knowing that would be the last time she would see her innocent face. She took relief somehow in knowing that Tommy was controlling her destiny and prayed she wouldn't awaken to see her fate. Then Joe and Fred grabbed Sherry up and drug her out to a front porch.

They sat her on a chair and Joe said, "You're going to watch this, you bitch, before you die."

She looked around to see nothing, but desert in all directions as far as the eye could see.

"This is how it works." Joe said as he glanced back toward Jane. "I am going to fire one bullet into the air." Then he pointed to Jane. "This retard will have one hour to make her way out into the desert and try to make an escape." He laughed, "Retards are never smart enough to escape." The other three men laughed with him. He continued, "After one hour, we are going to hunt her and did I mention that we are going to kill her?"

He looked at Sherry and said, "This is a great training exercise. It teaches us our strengths and our weaknesses for when we are on the job. The world has too many retards anyway."

Sherry hated him more than she had ever imagined she could hate anyone. She was no longer afraid of him. She had been pushed to a point that she didn't know existed. She no longer felt pain or agony, she could only feel hate and anger.

Joe and his friends were chugging beers and then throwing the empty cans into the air to shoot at them. Jane sat in the dirt at their feet, crying. Each time they shot at a can, she would cover her ears. She seemed so small and fragile. Sherry's heart ached that she couldn't protect her any longer. She wished for her own death to come as to avoid watching.

She could barely keep her eyes open as she struggled to stay awake. Joe grabbed her hair and jolted her face toward his. He said, "Now, now this won't be much fun if you're not watching. I might be forced to make it a short exercise and not give her the full hour. I have to be back to work tomorrow and I am feeling a little tired and bored now." She wanted to throw up but fought the urge.

They placed Jane in the dirt and turned her to face forward toward the dessert.

"Listen to me you little retard. When you hear the next gun shot, that is when it is your time to run. You have one hour to make it out before we begin to hunt you." Joe said. He spoke slowly as to taunt her. She turned to look at Sherry sadly with tears in her eyes.

Sherry mouthed the words, "I love you. Run, please, run."

The gunshot sounded off and she turned one more time to Sherry and then began running. She was struggling to run as her leg would never allow a fast sprint. She tripped several times and fell before she was out of the distance for their eyes to watch. Sherry knew she would never see her again and that hurt more than any pain that they could ever scourge upon her.

Fred turned to Joe and said, "Well, should we go ahead and bury this one?"

"No, not yet, I want her to see her retarded friend dead when we bring her back. We can bury them together that way we will only have to dig one hole for the two pieces of shit." Joe replied.

They laughed together again as Fred said, "I think I will grab us some more beer from the cooler." They tossed down beer after beer during the hour that Jane was granted. Joe sat beside Sherry on the arm of the chair and said, "I want you to know that this hurt me more than it hurts you." The laughter echoed in her brain.

The hour came to pass and three of the men set out to find Jane. Fred was left to guard Sherry. They made a deal that whomever finds and kills her, the other two had to buy dinner for him the next night. Sherry sat on the porch all afternoon waiting for one of them to return carrying her dead body. As dusk began to set in, Joe returned first, he was empty handed.

"Well, looks like I will be buying someone dinner tomorrow night." Joe said before he got in his car and drove away, saying he wasn't waiting since he had an early shift the next morning. He leaned in and kissed Sherry before he left.

"I hope my next wife is a little less nosy. Well, I am going to leave you here to die now bitch." Joe stood up and walked away without even looking back. Sherry wondered how he could be so cold after having claimed to love her day after day for so long.

Sherry watched into the distance for one of the others to be seen carrying Jane's dead body until she could no longer see due to darkness. Fred sat outside with her taunting her from time to time.

"Poor little retard doesn't even stand a chance." Fred said.

The smaller man with dark hair was next to return empty handed. Fred seemed a little more nervous this time as he informed the man that Joe had already returned empty handed and left for home.

"Do you think we should call Mark or Joe and let them know?" The man asked.

Sherry immediately knew when he said the name Mark that Mark was involved in this also. He was Joe's best friend that she had met several times. He was also married, but he had children as well. His wife would be devastated as well to hear of this and she would probably be killed as well.

The two of them were growing increasingly anxious awaiting the return of the last man. It was very late and he had not returned. The two men began arguing about what to do. One of them was wanting to go ahead and bury Sherry and the other was wanting to go out and search in darkness.

After they argued in front of her for several minutes, Fred said, "We will wait until daylight then do a quick search. If we don't find the girl then we will go ahead and bury her." Pointing to Sherry.

The other man replied, "Sam might have gotten lost trying to carry her back. I guess you're right. We should wait at least until morning before we bury this cunt."

Fred opened another can of beer and said, "It's a damn shame that cellular service doesn't work out here."

Sherry silently prayed that Tommy had carried Jane to safety. She felt as if she could barely hold her head up and watched the flies enjoy their meal as they feasted on her blood stained bandaged finger. Her lips felt swollen, cracked and sore, she could still taste the blood if she licked them.

Fred turned to the other guy and said, "Let's throw this bitch back in the room, I'm tired."

The other guy said, "Let's just throw her on the couch. She will probably be dead by morning anyway. It isn't like she can get up and make a run for it."

Fred shrugged as they each grabbed a shoulder and drug her into the living room, tossing her on the couch. The cushions felt soft to her as she landed on her back. She felt as If she could sleep there and she would pray that she wouldn't wake up.

The two men went into the kitchen adjacent to the living room. She could hear the banging dishes and assumed they were preparing themselves something to eat.

She dozed off and when was woke up, Fred was sitting in a chair not far from her watching television. He had it turned to cartoons and was laughing like a child. She heard the toilet flush from down the hallway as the footsteps of the other man drew nearer. He stopped in front of the television and announced he was going outside to watch a little longer for Sam and would be in shortly. Fred nodded and gestured at him to move. Sherry had no idea what time it was, but felt it had to be after midnight.

Sherry listened to the cartoons and Fred laughing as he continued to pop open beer cans. The other man still hadn't returned. Fred didn't seem concerned. Sherry listened for the door, intently wondering why the other man still had not returned. She heard Fred turn off the television and his footsteps following toward the back of the house. She felt as If he was going to lie down and go to sleep.

Sherry had dozed off and was awoken to the door opening and the other man staggering through, holding his throat with both hands. He appeared to be choking at first until she noted the blood pooling around his hands. He began to stagger toward her and fell on his face just before reaching the couch that she was laying on. There was a loud crash as he struck the coffee table, causing the beer cans stacked on it to fall. She noted Jane behind him darting toward the kitchen.

Fred came stumbling toward Sherry half-awake yelling, "What the fuck is going on in here." He noted his partner in the floor then leaned down and rolled him over to see his throat was cut. He turned directly to Sherry and said, "What the fuck did you do? You fucking bitch, I'll kill you now." He reached to grab her throat with his hands and began choking her as he climbed on top of her limp body. She was so weak that she didn't even try to fight. His face was red with anger as he squeezed tightly on her throat. Suddenly, his expression changed, his eyes widened as he lost his grip. His body became limp as his head fell to the right of Sherry's as he lay on top of her. Sherry noted Jane behind him stabbing him over and over with a large butcher knife. She continued to stab him as his body began to slide off onto the floor striking the small table that held the lantern.

The lantern fell to the floor as its fluid drained out and sat the rug on fire. The fire began to quickly spread and Jane took no notice and continued to stab the man. Sherry tried to raise up and couldn't muster the strength. Sherry tried to call out to her but her words were but a whisper. The flames were growing larger around them when Jane took note and ran to her. She tried to help her up, but she was too small to bare her weight.

Sherry whispered, "Jane, leave me here and get the keys from his pocket." Sherry watched as Jane quickly fumbled both dead men's pockets for keys. Jane turned to her as she dangled a set she had found.

She came back to Sherry's side and said, "I didn't do all of this for nothing, get up." Sherry tried again as Jane helped her and was able to sit then placing the majority of her weight on Jane they made their way out of the burning hell that they had been sentenced to.

Sherry still doesn't know how that tiny little girl was able to carry her out of that burning house. She still doesn't know how that tiny little girl was able to survive the desert and kill three hunters. It seems inconceivable that she could have even survived until dark.

She helped her into the small truck that was parked outside then ran around and put herself in the driver's seat.

Sherry whispered, "Jane, can you drive?"

"No." Jane shook her head as tears rolled down her face. Suddenly, she turned to Sherry again and said, "But I can drive." In Tommy's voice.

Sherry smiled as she wondered who really killed those men, Tommy or Jane. It really didn't matter because she was glad they were dead.

They had no idea which direction to go. Tommy followed the road until it met a black top road some miles later. He turned to her and said, "Left or right?"

"Right, because we are going to be alright." Sherry smiled. She didn't know which way to go, but she had to believe in something.

They turned right and drove for miles and miles before they began to see other headlights.

She whispered to Tommy, "Call David as soon as we get to a hospital. 805-226-9087 remember that, 805-226-9087" He repeated the number to her over and over as they drove in darkness.

She was awoken to Tommy calling out, "I see lights and we're going to be in a city." She tried to look out but couldn't raise her head. He said, "Please, please don't die now. We have come too far for you to quit now."

"I refuse to let them win. I am not going to die today." She wanted to believe her own words, but feared the infection in her finger had spread into her blood stream. She had struck a fever and felt as if she was burning up.

"It's Tucson, we are in Tucson." Tommy announced.

"Watch for the exit to the hospital."

They drove for what seemed a long time before he slowed to take an exit. He turned to her and said, "We are almost there, 805-226-9087"

She nodded and said, "First thing, call David."

"Okay." He said as he pulled into the emergency room entrance. He was honking his horn. Her door was flung open and two nurses eased her out onto a wheelchair. She couldn't sit up so one held her in the chair as the other one pushed it. They seemed to be moving quickly and she wanted to throw up.

That's the last thing she would remember about that night. She awoke several days later in a hospital bed with Jane and David at her side.

Jane ran to her side as soon as she opened her eyes and said, "See, you made it." She hugged Sherry as she whimpered with pain from her weight but pulled her closer.

David smiled and came closer as he grabbed her hand and said, "I should have listened to you that day and we should have never split up, I'm sorry."

Sherry said, "No, it's not your fault. Please don't blame yourself." She fought back tears as she said, "Did the police arrest Mark and Joe?"

David said, "Maybe we should let you get some more rest for now. We can discuss all of this later, right now you need rest."

"No, tell me now. Did they arrest them?"

He shook his head and said, "Not yet, I'm sorry." She turned her head to cry as Jane held her hand.

She had three cracked ribs and a broken arm. They had ran a rape kit and ended up having to take her finger off at the second knuckle through surgery. She was banged and bruised throughout her entire body. She was severely dehydrated and the mental damage would linger forever.

Sherry asked Jane, "Did the police talk to you?"

"Yes, they asked me what happened and I told them what I remembered." Jane answered.

"What do you remember Jane?"

"The only thing that I remember is that you and I were playing dominoes. I remember some men breaking in our door and putting bags over our heads then being in a room locked up." She stopped and wiped her tears.

Sherry said, "Do you remember anything else Jane?"

She nodded and said, "No, the last thing I remember is being in that little dark room with you and we were scared."

"It's not your fault Jane, none of this is your fault."

Jane nodded.

David said, "The police have been waiting to talk to you."

"I am ready whenever they are." Sherry nodded.

He said, "I am sure they will come today. The nurse said that she had notified them that you were awake."

Sherry had never felt so consumed with hate. She didn't realize that a person was capable of feeling as much hate as she felt.

Later that afternoon, a tall, thin, balding older man entered her room. He was wearing a suit with black shiny dress shoes. He knocked once on her open door then welcomed himself in.

He said, "Hello, my name is James Caldwell and I am with the Arizona State Criminal Investigations Division."

Sherry said, "I have been waiting for you."

He said, "Great, I want to hear what happened."

She started at the beginning and told the entire story. He took notes and asked a few questions along the way.

He said, "When I questioned Jane, she wasn't able to give much information, but that is not uncommon when someone had been through such a traumatic event." Then he said, "I however, cannot fathom how this tiny girl that doesn't weigh over 90 pounds was able to fend off and kill three men and carry you out of that cabin."

Sherry said, "I don't know how she did it either but it's the truth."

He turned away as if he was in disbelief with his lips perched. He thanked her and began to walk away stating, "I will be back in touch."

Sherry said, "Wait a minute."

He stopped and turned toward her. She said, "All of you are the same. You come here with your fancy suits and ties acting as if everything we say is a lie. I am telling you the truth and they are still out there waiting to finish what they started. They have killed others and will kill more and not even one of you give a shit. Do you really think that I could make this stuff up?"

"We are waiting on your rape kit and once we have the DNA results, we will be able to move forward. The bodies of the two men have been sent to the crime lab and we are still searching for the third body. Now, as far as Mark and Joe we have already talked to them. They both have alibis that they were at work during the times you were kidnapped, but if it comes back their DNA, that is another story."

Sherry said, "They couldn't have been at work during that time."

"I am sorry, but it was verified with their department."

"Of course it was, their department is in on it."

He leaned in toward her and said, "I want to help you and I do believe you, but we have to have some concrete evidence in order to convict. Do you have anything else to give me?"

She wiped her tears away and said, "That police department has been killing handicapped children for over 20 years. They use them as a training exercise and hunt and track them as if they are wild animals. They kill them and hide the evidence. If you walk away from this and allow it to continue, then you have to live with the guilt of knowing that you didn't do anything to help.

He turned nodded his head in agreement and said, "I will be back shortly.

Sherry turned to David and said, "Do you think he is going to help us?"

David shrugged his shoulder and said, "I don't know what to think anymore."

She dozed off and was awoken a few hours later by the same detective.

He said, "I have the results of the rape kit and neither, Mark or Joe raped you."

Sherry said, "I figured as much, they are very experienced at playing their games."

"Listen, I know that you don't trust me to investigate this fairly, but I do believe you and I do want to help you. I had a friend run a check in our database and over 20 handicapped girls and boys and have been either killed or murdered in this area in the last 10 years."

"So, what do we need to do?"

"Give me some time and let me see what I can come up with."

"What do we do in the meantime?" David asked.

He said, "We need to find a safe place for you somewhere."

Sherry turned to David as she felt they had exhausted all options. David said, "I have one more place we can go to."

Sherry sighed a little relief in believing that someone was willing to believe them and maybe even help them. Jane never left the hospital for the following six days that she was admitted. David would leave, but only briefly and state that he was preparing their new place of residence.

On the day of her release, the detective came to gather more information. He informed them that he couldn't tell them much, but he had uncovered a discrepancy in Mark's story and was currently investigating. Sherry felt as if she wanted to celebrate a victory then reminded herself how slick he was.

The investigator left his phone number and said, "Contact me immediately if you remember anything else and even if you just want to follow up."

Chapter 6

David helped her to the car and the three of them were on their way to a house that he said his parents owned when he was a child. It was on the outskirts of Phoenix and he felt it would be safe at least for the time being. They drove for over an hour and arrived at a small older home that appeared unkept and dilapidated.

He smiled and said, "I'm sorry, I know it's not much but at least it is safe, for now."

Sherry smiled and said, "It's perfect."

"I had the utilities turned on a few days ago and was praying that everything still worked."

It was a small house with two bedrooms, but thankfully the beds and couch were still in the house.

David had stocked the refrigerator and cabinets with food and said that he felt they should be okay for a number of days. Sherry eased herself onto the couch as Jane ran about exploring the house. David prepared them some tea and sat beside her on the chair.

He said, "So, what do we do now?"

She nodded and said, "I honestly don't know."

"I have a connection at my law firm that said he believes he can get us in to see Brittney at the River Bend Mental Institution. The thing is, we will have to go in as plumbers. My friend owns the plumbing company that services that hospital and they call frequently for stopped up drains and what not. I am just not sure how we can find out what room she is in."

Sherry sighed and said, "I am sure her brother will not give out that information." She widened her eyes and said, "Maybe Mrs. Hill can help us with that."

"How?"

"Walter visits Mrs. Hill often and she could ask him. I am sure he would tell her, he seems to care about her."

David said, "I think we need to pay Mrs. Hill another visit."

Sherry smiled and said, "I believe so."

Jane fell asleep on the couch that night watching television. Sherry turned to David and said, "Why haven't you asked me yet?"

"Asked you what?"

"Why Jane doesn't remember much about our ordeal?"

He shrugged his shoulders and said, "I assume her brain blocked it out."

"No, David that is not it." She leaned in toward him and said, "Jane wasn't with me throughout that ordeal, Tommy was. Tommy saved my life. Tommy carried me out of that cabin and Tommy killed those men."

His eyes widened as he said, "I hadn't thought of that."

"I begged him not to leave and allow Jane to endure the pain." She wiped a tear as she said, "He stayed with me the entire time."

"I am grateful to Tommy for what he did." He nodded his head as he said, "My worst fear right now is that this will not end the way that we want it to."

"I have the same fear but we have gone too far now and it is too late to turn back."

He nodded and said, "I feel the same way."

Before they left the house that morning David said, "I want to show you both something before we leave." He motioned for them to follow him into the kitchen. He pulled back on the refrigerator and exposed a small trap door. He said, "This was a safe area that my father had pointed out to us as children. If something ever happens at this house, this is where you need to hide." He showed them how to hide in the small area and then grab the back of the refrigerator and pull it back to make it appear as if it had never been moved.

The next morning, Sherry announced to Jane that they were going to pay Mrs. Hill a visit and she couldn't have been happier. She was ready and standing at the door impatiently long before they were ready. They were on the road by eight that morning as Jane watched for punch buggies along the trip. They arrived to find Mrs. Hill on the porch watching the cars pass by.

She waved, smiling as Sherry got out of the car. She noted Jane and almost fell coming down the few porch steps to greet her. She hugged Jane as if she had known her a lifetime.

"My goodness, what a wonderful day this has turned out to be." Mrs. Hill said.

Sherry said, "How have you been?"

"The same I reckon, but it don't look like you're doing well." As she pointed to her bandaged finger.

Sherry said, "Oh, a little accident in the kitchen, no big deal."

Mrs. Hill invited them in as Sherry introduced her to David.

Mrs. Hill said, "It's always nice when you come by, but even nicer when you bring Jane." Smiling.

Sherry said, "We always enjoy seeing you as well Mrs. Hill."

She asked Jane to help her make our tea as they headed off toward the kitchen. David walked about the room studying the pictures of Tommy and Jake as children that decorated her living room.

They returned with the tea and as they sipped it Mrs. Hill said, "I suppose you have some more questions for me?"

"Mrs. Hill I don't want you to feel like we only visit you to gather information." Sherry reassured her.

"That is not what I meant, I am sorry." She sighed and said, "If I can help find out what happened to Tommy then I am at your disposal."

Sherry said, "Has Walter visited you lately Mrs. Hill?"

"He called me yesterday and said that he had some fresh tomatoes he was going to bring by tomorrow afternoon."

"That's wonderful."

Mrs. Hill nodded and said, "Why do you ask?"

Sherry said, "We found out that his sister is at the River Bend Mental Institution with a strict visitation list. We want to speak with her but can't. I was hoping you could find out what room she is in."

"I can try but no guarantees. He might tell me and he might not."

"Maybe if you approach it as if you want to write her letters to make her feel better then he would give it to you."

Mrs. Hill nodded and said, "Maybe, I am sure she doesn't get many letters or visitors and she did know me quite well." She smiled and said, "I'll give it one hell of a try."

They visited most of the day and it felt so nice to have human interaction outside of their trio. Jane and Mrs. Hill played cards and looked at old photographs. Mrs. Hill was always so excited to spend time with Jane. It seemed she glowed with excitement when Jane was near. They left that afternoon with the hopes that she would be calling them with more information the next day.

Once they arrived back at the old house, there wasn't much to discuss. They fixed a quick dinner then Jane went into the living room to watch television. David and Sherry stayed in the kitchen to clean up. She was washing dishes and he was drying and putting them away.

She stopped and said, "David, you must regret that you ever got involved in this?"

He smiled and said, "I regret that I didn't follow through with it years ago."

"This has been the biggest trial of my life. I know I cannot stop and that I have to either finish it or it finish me."

"Yes, they would never leave us alone now."

The next morning David said, "I am going to give the detective a call and let him know we are okay and see if he has any updates." He dialed the number on the card and asked, "Yes, could I speak to detective Caldwell please?" His mouth dropped as he turned toward Sherry with phone in hand. He said, "Okay, thank you." He slowly lowered his phone while he gazed into her eyes.

She said, "What is it?"

"James Caldwell was shot in a drive by shooting last night." Chills ran up her spine and a coldness swept through her body.

"Is he dead?"

David nodded his head and said, "I don't know, they wouldn't say anything other than he was shot."

"We need to go back to the state police and let them know about this case."

He said, "I agree, if he was shot then it had something to do with us.

They drove back to that state police that morning and they were told to wait as they brought a different detective to speak with them. They explained their case and then he excused himself to pull their file. He was a young man in his late twenties and he was tall. He had dark hair with bright blue eyes. He introduced himself as Aaron Schultz. He seemed eager to listen to them. He said that Mr. Caldwell had trained him three years ago when he came to the department. He said that Mr. Caldwell was in ICU and it was not known if he would survive. He promised to look into the case and seemed interested in their story.

On the drive back to their house that afternoon, Sherry watched out the window in silence as the sadness consumed her in knowing that someone else might die due to this investigation. She knew they had to stop it but she didn't know what else she could do.

They arrived back at the house and Sherry felt exhausted. Her finger still ached as she realized that it would be a constant reminder for the rest of her life of this tragedy, if she manage to survive it. David's phone rang and he quickly answered it. He stepped outside for a few minutes to speak with whomever it was then came back into the living room with a half-smile.

Sherry said, "Who was it?"

He said, "My friend at the plumbing company said that they have an appointment for tomorrow afternoon at the River

Bend Mental Institution. They want their pipes inspected due to lack of water pressure."

"That is great! I hope Mrs. Hill can help us find out her room."

"If not, we will go anyway and hope for a miracle."

She nodded.

That afternoon, they hadn't heard from Mrs. Hill so Sherry called her in anticipation. She answered, "Hello."

"It's Sherry, did Walter come by?"

"Yes, he did but I couldn't get the room number out of him. He seemed suspicious after he told me that she was on the second floor. He said he would take me to visit if I wanted. I agreed to a visit tomorrow."

Sherry said, "That is wonderful, what time?"

"Two O'clock."

"Mrs. Hill, I can't explain everything right now but I promise I will later. If you see me or David there then please do not act as if you know us."

"Who are you?" Mrs. Hill joked.

Sherry slightly chuckled and said, "Thank you."

David said, "There is one more problem."

"What?"

"Jane, she is too small to dress up and go in as a plumber and we shouldn't leave her alone."

"You're right, we can't do that. Only one of us should go in and I feel like she might respond better to a woman." He nodded as Sherry said, "I'll go in, I'll watch and wait for Walter and Mrs. Hill to leave and then I'll go in."

He said, "You have got to be very careful not to get caught."

The next afternoon, Sherry left in David's car at noon. She arrived at River Bend and noted the Plumbers truck in the back of the building.

She approached them and a heavy set, short older man said, "You must be Sherry."

"Yes."

He said, "I need you step into the back of this van and put this on." Handing her a set of coveralls with their company logo. "Just follow along with us until we get past the front reception area."

She nodded and stepped into the van the slip on the coveralls then came out watched them gather their tools.

Within a ten minutes, they proceeded toward the front doors. She had a cap on and had put my hair up in it. She had worn some clear eyes glasses as well in hopes that the lady at the front desk would not recognize her from her visit before. They arrived at the front reception area and the receptionist didn't even look up. She was on the phone and motioned them on past. They got on the elevator and proceeded to the second floor. Once they arrived on the second floor, Sherry noted Mrs. Hill right away with Walter walking down the hallway and entering the last room on the left. She followed the plumbers into another room and occasionally peaked out awaiting their departure.

An hour later, she noted them to leave. She told the heavy man that she needed to go to the room at the end of the hallway. He walked with her toward the room at the end of the hallway and once they entered he said, "Okay, now when I get back to the other room I want you to turn the water on."

She noted Brittney sitting in a wheel chair staring out the window and seeming to not acknowledge her in the room.

She proceeded toward her and said, "Brittney, I am Sherry. I came to see you."

Brittney turned toward her and Sherry noted the dark circles under her eyes appeared to be almost black. She said, "What do you want?"

"I married Joe Masters and now I believe he is a killer." Sherry answered.

Brittney smirked and said, "That will get you killed, or worse."

Sherry said, "I need to know what happened to you."

She sighed and said, "Why, so you can confirm I'm crazy? They have already done that."

"No, no, I want to help you."

"You can't help me, no one can help me. You should help yourself and stop what you are doing."

"I can't, I've come too far. Please, tell me."

She shook her head and said, "Get out of here, I won't be a party to another death."

"If you don't help me then that is exactly what you will be a party to. There is a young handicapped girl that is going to be killed unless you help me."

She fought back tears and said, "That's what happened to Stephanie. They killed her. I watched in horror as they killed her. When I refused to keep quiet about it, they wanted to kill me, but they knew that Walter would tell so they agreed to commit me instead. My own brother testified against me and said that I was delusional"

Sherry said, "What happened that night?"

"We had a dance at the school. Stephanie came with Tommy to the dance, but Mark and Joe were having fun showing off in front to their friends dancing with her. They were taunting her and she didn't even know it. Their friend Fred wanted to go to an area outside of town and have a bonfire and drink some beers so they invited some of us along. Walters's girlfriend wanted to go and he didn't. She enjoyed feeling like she was part of the popular kids group. He finally agreed to go. Stephanie wanted to go and Tommy didn't. They argued for a few minutes when Walter's girlfriend offered Stephanie a ride. Walter allowed her to go even though he knew that they were going to make fun of her. He did whatever Jenny wanted, he was afraid she would break up with him I guess."

"What happened once you got to the bonfire?"

She moistened her lips to proceed, "The guys had parked their trucks to form an open circle in the center of them. They had brought out their speakers from the back of their trucks and were playing loud music. Some of them had spot lights and were shining them on the circle in the center as they took turns dancing in the circle."

She stopped and shook her head as if the memory was still etched into her brain. "Once they noticed us, they immediate started applauding. Joe said he had been waiting for Stephanie. She seemed excited that he would even talk to her, much less want to dance with her. She darted toward him as they proceeded to dance in the circle. They were flashing their spot lights off and on as if they were strobe lights and I could tell that it was making Stephanie uncomfortable. She tried to walk out of the circle and Joe grabbed her and drug her back in as laughter ensued. Joe began spinning her in circles as she began to cry. Walter asked him to stop but he shoved him back, knocking him down.

I still remember the look on Stephanie's face. It was horror, pure horror. The drinking was heavy that night. They were popping open beer after beer. Stephanie wanted to go home and she begged Walter after she had begun to vomit. Walter called out to them and wanted to go home. Joe wasn't ready. Mark approached us and started calling Walter a pussy. Jenny refused to leave too. I was talking with one of my friends, her name is Julia and she wasn't comfortable with what was going on. She had come with her boyfriend, Jess. He was a few years older than the rest of us.

I suppose he also became uncomfortable with the situation. He offered me to go with them but I felt like I had to stay and watch out for Walter and Stephanie. The party lasted for hours, we had arrived around nine and it was approaching two that morning. They were still drinking and dancing. Stephanie was still being made to dance off and on for their entertainment. Mark and Joe were taking turns with her. She was so tired she was being tossed about like a rag doll. My heart ached for her but what could I do?" Brittney had tears rolling down her cheeks.

Sherry said, "How did they kill her?"

"Walter was sitting on the hood of his truck staring toward his girl, Jenny. She was drunk too and had been talking to Fred for over an hour. I could tell that he was heartbroken. I sat beside him and we began to talk. Suddenly, I noticed Stephanie was no longer in the circle and Mark and Joe had disappeared as well. We began to search for them, their trucks were still there."

"Where were they?" Sherry asked.

"The party had grown thin, everyone had left or were leaving. Walter was upset because Jenny had left with Fred and he wanted to leave. We couldn't find Stephanie after searching for more than 30 minutes, but we couldn't find Joe or Mark either. It was dark and we didn't have a flash light. We came back to find the trucks still there. We knew that something bad was happening, we could feel it. We waited for over an hour on the hood of Walter's truck." She wiped her tears, "Out of the darkness they emerged. Joe was carrying Stephanie's limp body as Mark trailed beside him. They were staggering from the alcohol they had consumed and the laughter rang through to my brain.

I asked them what they did. Joe tossed her body to the ground like it was one of his empty beer cans. I noticed blood on her panties as her dress rose up when she fell. Joe grabbed me by my throat and threatened me. He shoved me back as he released my throat. I fell to the ground in horror looking toward my brother."

She turned her head the other way and said, "My pussy brother was worried about the trouble we would be in. Mark demanded Walter to help clean up the mess. Joe accused Walter of raping Stephanie."

She stopped and cleared her throat and said, "I had a history of drug use and was known for being an introvert. My parents had me medicated and they had diagnosed me as a child as being delusional with paranoid schizophrenia. I suppose Walter realized that he was going to have to give in to their commands or else risk the alternative." She turned to me in seriousness and said, "I am assuming you already know that every one of them had a parent in law enforcement. Walter was told to take her body to dispose of it. They told him to frame Jake. I suppose they chose him because they hated him and because he was known for his attitude and previous arrest record. They told him if he ever told anyone that they would swear it was him that did it and they would kill me.

When we arrived at Jakes house, Walter instructed me to wait in the truck. He grabbed Stephanie's body that was wrapped in a black trash bag. He carried it towards Jake's car and grabbed his key to open the trunk." She stopped and said, "You see, Jake had given my brother a key to his car because they were like brothers and Walter could take his car anywhere he needed anytime he needed. I watched as he lifted the trunk to place her body inside. Then I turned because a shadow caught my eye and I saw Tommy standing outside in the darkness watching Walter. I panicked and waited but Tommy never moved. He watched in silence."

She cried out loud and said, "I should have never told Walter that Tommy was out there that night. I was freaking out when he got back in the truck, I was hysterical. I told Walter that Tommy had seen what he did. I wanted to go to the police. I trusted my brother and never dreamed what he would do next."

Sherry said, "What did he do?"

She said, "He." She stopped and a nurse entered the room.

The nurse said, "Can I help you?"

"Oh, no I am sorry. I was just asking this lady which side of the sink the hot water is on." Sherry said.

The nurse said, "They should be marked." questionably.

Sherry smiled and said, "I think we got it now." Sherry proceeded past her to exit the room.

"Excuse me ma'am, can I ask your name?" The nurse asked.

Sherry kept walking as if she didn't hear her. Sherry told the heavy man she was leaving and made a fast pace out of the building.

Sherry arrived back at the house to find David and Jane playing cards. She was anxious to tell David what she had learned.

"Before you say anything, I have something to tell you." David said.

She said, "Okay?"

"Mr. Caldwell passed away this morning. Detective Aaron Schultz called to tell me and he said that he also believes that it has something to do with our case. He wants to meet with us tomorrow."

Sherry sat down slowly in realizing that if Mr. Caldwell had never met them then he would still be alive today.

Sherry said, "I am sorry to hear about Mr. Caldwell, I feel horrible for his family."

"I know, I do too. Were you able to find Brittney and speak with her?"

Sherry smiled and said, "Yes, she told me everything. I think I know why Walter is the way he is now."

Sherry told him everything that Brittney had shared with her.

He listened intently and said, "The problem is that no one will believe Brittney. She has probably told that story a million times and no one believes her. We still have to prove it."

Sherry nodded and said, "I know, but how?"

Jane spoke but in Tommy's voice, "I do remember seeing Walter put a bag in Jake's trunk but I didn't know what it was."

Sherry turned to see that Jane was standing just outside the bedroom door where they were talking. Sherry said, "Tommy, I am sorry. I didn't mean for you to hear our conversation."

He said, "They killed Stephanie and put her in a plastic bag? Then they made Walter put her in my brother's trunk?"

Sherry nodded and said, "I'm sorry Tommy, but yes that is what they did."

He started pacing three steps right, three steps left, saying over and over, "That's bad, that's bad." He had his head in his hands and was nodding back and forth.

Sherry said, "Tommy, please stop and listen to me." He wouldn't stop. She went to him and placed her hands on his shoulders. She said, "Please Tommy, stop and listen to me."

He stopped and looked to her through glazed eyes and said, "They killed Stephanie."

Sherry said, "They did, and we are going to make them answer for it."

They spent most of the evening trying to calm Tommy down. He was very upset and Sherry felt terrible that he had been able to sneak and listen to their conversation. She had always tried to be careful as to not let him or Jane overhear their conversations. It was late before they were able to go to sleep that night. Sherry awoke first the next morning and decided to cook everyone some pancakes for breakfast. David was next to emerge from his bedroom. He seemed pleased to smell the pancakes and bacon.

Sherry said, "I'm surprised that Jane isn't up yet." She had allowed her to sleep in the other bedroom and she had slept on the couch due to her having such a bad night.

Sherry went into the bedroom to awake her for breakfast and found an empty bed. She panicked and yelled, "David, she is not here!"

He burst into the room to see the empty bed as well. He said, "Where would she go?"

Sherry said, "She wouldn't go anywhere. She doesn't have anywhere to go."

They quickly began searching the house, every closet every bathroom. David ran outside to search the yard but she was nowhere to be found.

Sherry was imagining in her mind that Mark or Joe had snuck in and taken her while they slept. She kept thinking that she would have heard it, but maybe she slept through it. Her mind was running so fast that she couldn't even think straight.

David said, "Let's get in the car and drive the area."

Sherry agreed and they began their search but they didn't find her. Sherry was hysterical, she was trembling from fear imagining the tortures of that small cabin in the woods they had managed to escape. David was trying to reassure her and telling her that they would find her but he knew what they were capable of. Sherry felt as if she was gone forever and couldn't bare the pain. Her heart ached and she felt as if she had somehow failed to protect her.

She called Mrs. Hill and told her that Jane had disappeared and begged her to call if she showed up. She felt as if that was the only place that she would go if she had walked away on her own.

Mrs. Hill sounded distraught and promised she would call. David suggested that they follow through with their scheduled meeting with detective Schultz.

He said, "We will tell him of Jane's disappearance and hope that he can help."

Sherry agreed and they proceeded to the meeting. Sherry cried most of the drive and David tried to reassure her by stating, "Maybe she will be home when we get back." Sherry nodded, but she knew Jane wouldn't be there.

They met with the detective that afternoon and told him of the disappearance of Jane. He assured them that he would go check in on where both Joe and Mark were. He said that he would also put an APB out on Jane by giving her description and check with them that afternoon. Sherry was completely distraught. They left and drove straight back to their small home hoping to find Jane. They watched all along the way back. When they arrived back home she wasn't there much as Sherry had expected.

Later that afternoon, detective Shultz called and said that both Mark and Joe were working and had been for the last several days. He said that he would have some officers keep a watch on them, but he suspected that they had nothing to do with the disappearance of Jane. Sherry suggested that they could have other friends involved in it and he agreed and then stated that he was watching them.

It was frighteningly quiet that evening. Neither one had anything to say. It was a constant worry, wondering where Jane was and who had taken her.

David said, "Do you think it would help if we went back and talked to Walter?"

Sherry shook my head and said, "He isn't going to talk to us,"

"You're probably right, but just sitting here is eating away at me."

Sherry nodded and said, "We could go and follow them. See what they are up to?"

He nodded and said, "Yes, but what if we choose the wrong one to follow?"

"It seemed to me that that Mark and Joe were equally in charge and besides, now they lost three of their workers, thanks to Tommy."

"I figure if they took Jane then they are both behind it."

Sherry nodded and said, "Let's leave early and watch Joe's house."

He smiled and said, "I'll be up before daylight."

Sherry nodded and said, "As will I."

They left at four that morning and parked at a house less than half a block away to watch for him to leave. He emerged from his house around and five and left in his police cruiser. They followed him to the station. It appeared as if he was going to work as usual. They stayed parked in the back parking lot. Sherry noted Mark to arrive a few minutes later and go into the station. It appeared they were both working that day.

Sherry said, "They probably killed her right away and disposed of the body." Crying, she wiped her tears.

David said, "Now listen, we don't know that yet."

She nodded and said, "You're right. We can hope."

They both left in their police cruisers within an hour. They each had a younger appearing partner join them in their cruisers.

David said, "What do you want to do now?"

"I don't know. Maybe we should go see if Walter is working or anything looks odd at his trailer?"

They drove to his trailer and found his vehicle gone and then checked his work place and noted his car. They assumed he was working today as well.

Sherry said, "They must have others involved that were not there when they held me and Jane captive."

David said, "Do you think you could find the place where you were held?"

"No, I have no idea where it was."

They drove back to the house and anxiously waited to hear any news from anyone. The phone never rang the entire day.

That evening as Sherry was preparing to lie down, David said, "I want you to know something."

"What?"

"I want you to know that I will never regret this, no matter the outcome."

"That makes me feel a little better since I have ruined you're life."

He shook his head and said, "No, you didn't ruin my life. You showed me what it means to stand up and fight for what is right. I couldn't do that before and without you I never would have."

Sherry began crying and said, "What good has it done?"

He walked toward her and wrapped his arms around her. "I know how much it hurts to lose Jane, but if we stop them at least no one else will die at their hands. That has to mean something."

She wiped her tears and said, "Yes, it does." She stared into his eyes and said, "But, what if we don't stop them?"

"We will. I believe we will. I have to believe that we will."

Meanwhile, Jane was on the run and Tommy had his own agenda. He had taken a car that someone had left the keys in and he had tracked down the police station and watched as Mark and his partner pulled out of the building to protect the streets in their police cruiser. He followed him to a small coffee shop where the partner went inside and got them some donuts and coffee. He got out of the car and waited for him to come out of the coffee shop. When he made his exit, Tommy waited until he was almost to the bar and struck him with a baseball bat in the back of the head. He took his gun and jumped in and held it to Marks throat.

"What the fuck?" Mark said.

"Be quite my friend, it's time to pay for your sins." Tommy ordered him to drive slowly out of the parking lot.

It was early morning and still dark out so he had Mark pull into a dark alley way. He ordered him to stop and use his handcuffs and cuff both of his own hands to the wheel. He was sweating profusely as he already had the trigger cocked.

Tommy said, "Do you remember me?"

He nodded.

"I'm sorry, I couldn't hear you. I said, do you remember me?" Tommy asked louder.

"Yes, yes, I remember you."

"I have spent a lot of time thinking about what I would do to you if I were to ever see you again. I thought about killing you, but then again, that would be too easy for you. Then I thought, what would someone like you miss the most and it occurred to me." As he pulled out pliers from a bag, he laughed as he said, "This little piggy went to market." Cutting his left pinky off. He said, "This little piggy stayed home." Cutting his left ring finger off. Mark was screaming in horror as he watched his fingers be cut off, one by one. He collapsed as Tommy cut the third. Tommy hurriedly finished all ten then disappeared into the night.

A few hours later, Sherry and David were sitting on the couch. He leaned her over to place her head on his lap and began brushing her hair. Then his phone rang.

He quickly answered it and said, "Hello." Then motioned to Sherry mouthing the name "Detective Schultz".

She sat up and watched as David walked around the room saying, "Okay, yes, no, etc." Once the conversation ended he hung up and looked at her with wide eyes.

"What? Did they find her? Is she alive?" Sherry asked.

"I don't know."

"What did he say?"

"Mark was found injured and he has been taken to the hospital."

"What happened?"

"The partner in the cruiser with Mark told the police that he doesn't know what happened. He said that he went in a donut shot and came out and that is the last thing he remembers. He woke up in the hospital some time later."

"I would like to say that I am sorry to hear that but, I am not."

"They found Mark's cruiser in a back alley a few hours later and his hands were cuffed to the steering wheel."

"What?"

"Yes, but Sherry there is one more thing."

"What?"

"Mark's fingers, all ten, were cut off."

"Jane, Oh my god Jane." She cried, "David, do you think it was Jane?"

He said, "No, not Jane. It was Tommy. I believe it was Tommy."

Sherry's mind was running so fast that she couldn't think straight. If she went after Mark, she would go after Joe and probably Walter as well. She said, "David we have to do something."

"What?"

"I don't know, but we have to do something."

"Detective Schultz said that they are looking for her."

"Oh my god, I never thought that she would go after them. I am sure it is Tommy, but no one will ever believe that."

"I know, they will believe it was Jane."

She was shaking as she pranced back and forth across the living room floor. She said, "I don't know what to do."

"I don't either. I suppose we just have to wait now and hope that the police find her before she finds Joe."

Sherry was panicked, trembling and wanted to rush out and look for her. She said, "We have to go search for her. We have to find her."

"We can go drive and search for her if that is what you want to do."

"Please, let's go."

They drove most of the night and several times they thought they had spotted her, but each time it was someone that looked similar. They went back home and tried to sleep, but Sherry lay awake mostly, trying to sleep and hoping she would come back.

She was up making coffee when David walked in and said, "You couldn't sleep either?"

She nodded and said, "I just wish she would come back."

"You do know that if she comes back, they are going to expect her to answer for what she did to Mark."

Sherry nodded and said, "But you are a lawyer, you can help her right?"

"I will try, but no one is going to believe that she is possessed by a man that went missing 20 years ago."

Sherry didn't want to have to think about that right now. She wanted Jane to come back and we would figure that out later.

"I feel like she is going to go after Joe and maybe Walter."

"I do to, especially after overhearing us talking about Walter putting Stephanie's body in his brother's trunk."

She nodded and said, "Do you think that if we went to visit Mark he would talk to us?"

He shrugged his shoulders and said, "I highly doubt that even if his fingers are all cut off, he is going to answer questions that would lead to guilt."

"I know but he might describe the girl to us."

Maybe, but he will recognize us so, I believe that should be left to the detective. We could however pay a visit to the partner in the car with him and see if he would talk to us?"

"That is a wonderful Idea. How would we find out who he is?"

"I'll check with a friend of mine and find out if they can get some information." He walked outside and made a call as she watched him outside the window. He came back in and said, "She is working on it. She should know by the afternoon."

She nodded and said, "I believe Joe has spoken with Mark by now and he will be on the lookout for Jane. David, if he finds her before we do, he will kill her on the spot."

"I know and he might even suspect that it was you and be watching for you."

Sherry hadn't thought about that but David was right. It was possible that Joe will believe that she attacked Mark and be looking for her. She needed to stay hidden. She felt useless hiding in that house but knew that she needed to. Waiting was something that she was never very good at.

David said, "How about I make a quick trip into town and get us some more food. We can spend the day here going over all of our notes and findings and see if we missed something?"

"I would rather go with you."

"I feel that it would be safer here. We will just get by with what we have and I will stay here too."

"No it's fine, I will wait here. You go get the food and I will clean house while you are gone."

He gathered his things and was out the door in a matter of minutes. It was a 20 minute drive to the nearest grocery story and twenty minutes back. She would be alone for around an hour. He had been gone for only 15 minutes when she heard a thump at the side of the house. Her initial thought was that it could be Jane, but she didn't want to walk outside for fear that it wasn't. She couldn't see anyone out any of the windows as she crept about peeking out them.

Then it happened, someone kicked the front door open and rushed in. He had a gun in his hands and a mask over his face. He was a very tall man, well over six feet. He was hefty weighing in over 300 hundred pounds. She quietly slid the refrigerator out and hid in the small cubby hole behind out. Then she quietly slid the refrigerator back. She was confident that he hadn't spotted her as she noted him to walk towards the bedroom. She held her breath and tried to be silent. She could hear him kicking open doors and slamming things about.

Then she heard his footsteps come into the kitchen as he was opening cabinets and the closet. She even heard him open the refrigerator. He must have taken a drink from the refrigerator as she heard him pop the top of a can of soda or beer. She never heard him leave so she stayed crouched in the small area until she heard David call out some time later for her. He seemed frantic as he called out for her. She shoved the refrigerator back and emerged shaking and crying.

He ran to her and said, "What happened?"

She told him of the man kicking in the door with a gun.

David called Detective Schultz immediately and then said, "We cannot stay here anymore. Gather your things quickly."

They gathered a few things and were gone within minutes. She kept watching out the rear view mirror hoping that we were not being followed. She kept imagining Jane coming back to that house and finding they had gone. What would she think? What would she do?

David said, "Jane knows both of our phone numbers. She will call if she decides to talk to us."

She knew he was right but she also knew that she didn't have a phone.

They went to a motel located only blocks from the state police office. David called Detective Shultz and told him where they were. Detective Shultz came to their room within an hour.

"I have spoken with Mark and the woman that attacked him fits the description of Jane." Shultz sighed and said, "I know we cannot be certain it was her. The thing is, all leads point toward her. She had motive and she is missing. She is very small to be out there doing things like this and I have to wonder where someone that small in stature would get the strength needed to pull a stunt like this." Sherry didn't reply to him and instead decided to tell him of my visit with Brittney the day before Jane disappeared.

He listened intently as she recounted the story that Brittney had told. He said, "She has been declared legally insane. I believe the story, but it would be practically impossible to get a jury to believe her."

Sherry nodded and said, "I know that, but I believe she is telling the truth. I believe that she was wrongfully declared insane."

"That is something we can look at someday after we close this case, but right now we need to find Jane before she gets herself in more trouble."

"If Jane is the one that attacked Mark then she will go after Joe and Walter as well." Sherry said.

"I feel the same way and I have warned Joe. When I told him that I felt it was Jane, he didn't seem too concerned and said she is crazy asked me if he had the right to protect himself." He sighed and said, "Joe is going to kill her if he sees her. Then he will label it as self-defense."

Sherry began to sob and said, "We have to find her before they do."

The detective said, "Do you have any idea where she might be?"

"The only person that she knows and cares about besides David and myself is Mrs. Hill. I have already contacted her and she will call if she hears anything."

"Who is Mrs. Hill?"

"She is Tommy Hill's mother and Jane made friends with when we first began investigating the disappearance of Tommy Hill."

"Why did you begin investigating the disappearance of Tommy Hill?"

She stopped and turned to David. She didn't know what to say. David stared back at her, unsure himself. She said, "That is such a long story. I am not sure you want to hear it."

"I would like to hear it. Please tell me." He leaned back in the chair and crossed his legs.

Sherry turned to David and he nodded that she should tell the entire story. She began all the way back to where Jane had first arrived at the hospital having seizures up until now. She told him how Tommy had rescued her from that cabin and carried her out of the terror that night. He listened intently only asking a few questions.

When she had finished he sat silently for a moment and then said, "I don't know if I believe you or not. But, I do believe that you believe what you are telling me." He shook his head and said, "I can tell you that a juror will never believe that story."

She turned to wipe her tears.

He said, "The most important thing right now is that we need to find Jane. If you think of anything, anything at all then call me." He stood to walk away.

Sherry said, "Sometimes things happen for a reason. I didn't want to believe any of this either. I was married, happy and going forward in a life that I had only dreamed of. I sacrificed all of that to save lives, when so many had already been lost."

He turned back toward her and said, "I am sorry that this has happened to you, I truly am. I didn't say that I believe you are lying. I said I didn't know if I believe you or not. Only time will

172

tell the truth, but right now we need to focus on finding Jane."
He walked out the door.

Sherry was exhausted but she still I couldn't sleep. She
laid in the bed next to David's bed and tossed and turned. She
had been through so much and the anticipation of knowing
that it was going to be over riddled her with so many
unanswered questions. She knew if Jane died at the hands of
Joe then this nightmare would continue forever and she also
knew that she would have to hide forever. She felt so much
guilt for the lives they had destroyed and lost in the process.
David could never go back to his law practice and live a
normal life. Detective Caldwell was dead due to them
involving him and what about Doug, somewhere, someone
missed him and wanted to see him again. She was lying in
bed glaring at the ceiling crying when David crawled into the
bed beside her and wrapped his arms around her.

It felt good to be held and to feel safe. She hadn't had
that in so long, she had forgotten how it felt. He began kissing
her on her ear, then her neck then slowly working his way
down. She gave into his affections without even blinking an
eye. She was consumed with the feelings of being of
importance and meaning something to someone. It brought a
comfort to feel safe and secure with someone that must have
felt the same as her. They made love and slept in each other's
arms. They made no promises about tomorrow, mostly
because they couldn't. Tomorrow wasn't a promise that they
could keep.

Sherry awoke to note daylight behind their closed
curtains. She darted to the shower and readied herself for the
day. David was awake when she came out of the bathroom.
She was fearful that there was going to be an awkwardness
between them but much to her surprise, there wasn't.

He grabbed her and kissed her as he said, "It was wonderful last night and I want you to know that it wasn't out of fear, it was because I truly do care about you."

She smiled and said, "Thank you." He smiled back.

Chapter 7

They dressed and then sat in the room looking at the television unsure of what they should do.

Sherry said, "David, it has occurred to me that we keep asking ourselves where Jane would go. The one thing we have not asked ourselves is where would Tommy go?"

He turned his head to her and said, "You are right." As he stood up and walked toward her. "You are absolutely right. Where would Tommy go? There must be a place he liked to go to and play or hide from the world. We should call Mrs. Hill and ask her."

Sherry quickly grabbed her phone and then put it back down.

"What?" David asked.

"I can't ask her something like that. She wouldn't understand why I want to know."

He sat back down and said, "I hadn't thought about that."

"What about Jake? He would know of all of Tommy's little hideaways? We could visit him again and ask?"

"He will wonder why we are asking as well."

"Yes, but he might be able to handle the information a little better that Mrs. Hill if we tell the truth."

He nodded and said, "We are here anyway with nothing to do, let's go."

Tommy had been hiding near trash cans and eating out of them in dark alleys. He was so small that he could easily hide just about anywhere. He still carried his pliers in his little pink purse that Sherry had bought for him. He knew Joe's address as Sherry had written on several papers when he was admitted into the rehab. He was slowly making his way in that direction. He had come across a clothes line and managed to gain a new shirt and a hat to hide his hair. He was so entranced with vengeance he didn't realize the exhaustion that had consumed Janes small body.

He arrived at the small house around three that morning. He noted Joe's cruiser in the driveway and knew that he was home. He slowly tried each window, but they all seemed locked. He reached into his small pink purse and used the pliers to break the small bathroom window. He quickly went through it and was hiding in the kitchen closet, leaving it open a crack before Joe made his way in to see what the noise was all about. He watched through the crack as Joe turned on lights and began to search the house. He knew that it would only be seconds before Joe opened the closet he was hiding in. He had grabbed some insect spray from the closet and was armed and loaded.

Joe opened the closet and Tommy began spraying straight into his eyes. Joe fell back, grabbing his face. Tommy quickly grabbed a statue off the counter and slammed him in the head with it, twice. Joe lay unconscious on the kitchen floor as Tommy quickly grabbed his handcuffs that he had left on the table and cuffed him to the table legs he lay near. He took his night stick in case he were to come to before he could finish his task.

First, he quickly snipped off his fingers with the pliers. He turned to leave, then stopped and looked back with a hate in his eyes. He walked slowly back and veered at him bleeding on the floor. He leaned down and rolled him over slightly, then pulled his boxer shorts down enough to reveal his small limp penis. He leaned down with his pliers and with one clean snip it was gone. He tossed it to the wind as he made his way out of that small dark house.

Sherry and David had driven back to the prison near Tucson that morning. They were put on the list to visit at noon. They had two hours to kill while they waited so they drove to small coffee shop just a few miles away. They were sipping coffee when David's phone rang.

He looked at Sherry after checking his caller ID and said, "Detective Shultz." He answered, "Hello, yes." He listened for several minutes without speaking a word. Then he said, "Okay, thank you." He hung up the phone and stared wide eyed into Sherry's eyes without speaking a word.

"What, what is it?"

"It's Joe."

"What about Joe?"

"They found him in his kitchen floor this morning because someone called 911 to dispatch EMS. He is alive but," He stopped and turned away then said, "He was handcuffed to his kitchen and his penis was cut off, so were his fingers."

She gasped at the thought. She knew Jane had done this. "Oh my god David, Walter is next."

He nodded and said, "I think we need to pay Walter a visit this afternoon."

"What if he will not talk to us?"

"Then he will wish later that he had."

They drove back to the prison anxious to visit with Jake. The guards brought him to the glass window with the handset for us to speak with him. Sherry wasn't sure how to tell him of the events that had taken place. She began her story with Jane arriving at the hospital and told of every event.

He sighed and said, "Brittney is locked up, just like me for a crime we never committed."

Sherry said, "Brittney and you both could be freed if we can prove what really happened that night."

"My brother used to tell me all the time when we were kids that blood was thicker than water. I suppose I know now what he meant. He cannot rest as long as he knows the truth has yet to set us free."

Sherry nodded and said, "Jake, do you have any idea where he might go?"

"When we were kids there was an old tree house way back in the woods behind our house that we used to play in. Whenever Momma was mad at us and threatening to whip us we would hide out there. She knew where we were and would laugh about it later."

"Do you think he would go there?"

"I don't know where else he would go."

She thanked Jake and told him that they are working toward getting him set freed as well. They left knowing that they needed to find Jane and they needed to warn Walter.

David said, "I believe we need to warn Walter first?"

She nodded and said, "Hopefully Tommy hasn't already gotten to him."

They drove fast on the interstate and arrived back much quicker than they had anticipated. They first drove by Walter's trailer and noted that there were no cars there. Then they went to his shop, hoping to speak with him.

They walked toward the shop when Walter noted them and lunged toward them just outside the doors yelling, "I told you mother fuckers that I have nothing to say to you." He reeked of stale alcohol and his clothes were wrinkled and dirty. His eyes were bloodshot as if he had not slept in days.

Sherry said, "Walter, please you need to listen to us."

"I don't need to listen to anything you have to say. You need to get the fuck out of here before I call the police for harassment."

"Walter, you don't understand, you are in danger."

"Get the fuck out of here, now." She turned to walk away and he said, "You are a stupid bitch." He smirked and said, "You came here to tell me that I am in danger and you don't even have a clue about how much danger you are in."

She turned back toward him and said, "Yes, yes, I do. I know I am in danger but the real question is do you?"

He smirked and said, "I will just keep doing what I have had to do for so many years. Death might actually be a welcome addition with all that I have been through."

Sherry continued to walk slowly back to the car.

They drove away as Sherry turned to see Walter watching them. She thought to herself that this would probably be the last time that he would have to worry about them bothering him.

"David, do you think it would have helped if I had told him about Joe?"

"We couldn't even get a word in edgewise, how could we do that?"

"I don't know, I just feel like he needs to know."

David nodded his head and said, "You can't help people that will not help themselves."

They drove back toward Mrs. Hill's house and arrived to find her sitting on the porch. She was excited as always as Sherry emerged from the car. She greeted them with an anxiousness of information about Jane. She immediately detected my dark circles under Sherry's eyes and sensed something was wrong.

Mrs. Hill said, "Are you alright?"

Sherry nodded and said, "I have been under the weather a little lately and thought a trip out here might do me some good."

"Where is Jane? Did you find her?"

"I am sorry Mrs. Hill but she is still missing. We have looked everywhere that we know to look."

She looked down in sadness and said, "I pray that she is alright."

They followed Mrs. Hill into the house and she was making them a glass of iced tea before they could get seated.

"I have been worried to death about Jane. Where do you think she would go?" Mrs. Hill asked.

Sherry nodded and said, "I have no idea but we are trying to figure it out."

"It scares me to death to think about her being out there by herself somewhere. Have you called the police?"

"Yes, we have a missing person report out."

"Is there anything that I can do to help?"

"All that we can do at this point is pray." Sherry smiled.

Mrs. Hill appeared to try to hide her tears.

"Do you mind if we go for a walk?"

"Not at all, make yourself at home here." Mrs. Hill nodded

"I feel like a walk out here might do me some good."

Mrs. Hill nodded and said, "It might very well, it is quiet up here."

Sherry thanked her and turned to David as he got up to join her.

They walked outside and proceeded toward the back yard.

"Do you think she suspected anything?" Sherry asked.

David said, "No, she didn't appear to."

Sherry sighed, "Hopefully we can find this hideaway that Jake talked about."

David replied, "He said that it was a distance from the house. I suggest we search until we find it or dark whichever comes first."

She nodded.

They walked for over an hour in all directions trying to locate the small hideaway. They were beginning to lose hope when David called out to Sherry a few hundred feet from him. She joined him as he pointed to a small wood fort that was within eyes distance. She nodded as they began to approach it quietly. It was very small and only three four feet tall. It was poorly constructed, tattered and appeared to be made of scraps. They approached it with extreme caution as David leaned in to pull back the cloth door that hung over the entrance.

David called out, "Tommy, are you in there?" There was no reply. He pulled the curtain type door and peeked inside. He knelt down and began to crawl inside. Sherry followed.

Once inside, they noted open cans of potted mean and Vienna sausages that appeared to be fresh. There was an open bag of crackers and an old milk carton that was half full of tea.

Sherry said, "She has been here. David, she has taken food from Mrs. Hill's house and hiding out here."

David said, "She must be sneaking into the house after Mrs. Hill goes to bed."

Sherry nodded.

There was a blanket and pillow where she had been sleeping to avoid the elements and a black baseball cap that bore the emblem of their high school that Tommy was noted to be wearing in several of his photos that were displayed in Mrs. Hill's living room.

Sherry said, "Should we wait here and see if she comes back?"

David said, "I don't know, we could I guess, but how do we know she will come back before she attacks Walter?"

"Actually, we don't know who all is on the list of people to be attacked. I was wondering if she will go after some of the other people that were there that night."

"True, there were others there that night."

Sherry said, "Maybe we should call the detective and tell him what we found."

David nodded.

They walked back up to Mrs. Hill's house and thanked her for the nice visit then left there unsure what they should do. They decided to drive by Walter's house on the way back. They arrived to note that the lights were on but the car wasn't there.

Sherry said, "I wonder if that woman that lives with him is Jenny?"

David said, "Jenny is the girlfriend that insisted on going to that party and wouldn't leave?"

Sherry nodded.

David shrugged his shoulders and said, "She could be, we could ask. She didn't seem reluctant to speak with us."

David pulled into the driveway and honked his horn. The door opened and the woman with the tattoos opened the door and waved.

She walked out on the porch and said, "Can I help you?"

Sherry smiled at her as she got out of the car and said, "I am Sherry Masters, I came to speak with you if you don't mind."

The woman said, "I remember you from last week. Walter told you not to come around here anymore."

Sherry nodded and said, "That's right he did, but I didn't come to see Walter, I came to see you."

"What do you want?"

"Can I ask your name?"

"Why do you want to know my name?"

Sherry said, "It is important. I want to make sure you are the right person before I go any farther with my message."

"I am Jenny, Jenny Jones."

Sherry nodded and said, "I don't really know how to tell you this, but you could be in danger. I want you to know that you should leave this trailer and hide somewhere for a while."

Jenny laughed and said, "So, this is some sort of mental intuition that you had and I am supposed to be scared now?"

Sherry nodded and said, "Please, I am trying to help you, please."

Jenny laughed again and said, "Now, I am going to tell you the same thing Walter told you last week." She sighed, "Get the fuck off my property and do not come back here again." Shouting.

Sherry turned toward the car and looked at David. She began to walk slowly toward the car as the woman was laughing shaking her head.

Jenny said, "Crazy mother fuckers, they everywhere. Get help you stupid bitch."

Sherry got into the car as Jenny yelled, "Go on, and get the fuck out of here."

Sherry wiped her tear as it rolled down her cheek and said, "Let's go, she will know soon enough that she should have listened."

David said, "I hope not."

They drove away feeling as if they should have tried harder to convince her, but knowing she wouldn't have listened anyway.

Sherry said, "I wonder if Walter is still at work."

"Do you really want to try to talk some sense into him again?"

"I don't know, I don't know what to do."

He pulled the car over and turned toward her then said, "Listen, I know this is stressful for you, but we need to figure out what to do next."

She nodded and said, "Maybe she went back to the fort behind Mrs. Hill's house now."

"Maybe, but we don't know. I think we should call the detective and tell him about the fort behind Mrs. Hill's house."

She nodded and said, "Maybe you're right, maybe we should." He pulled his phone and dialed the number.

The detective wanted to meet with Sherry and David at Mrs. Hill's house. Sherry had no idea how she would explain this to Mrs. Hill, but she knew she had to try whatever she could to save Jane. They met the detective one hour later at Mrs. Hill's house and as David escorted Shultz and his partner into the woods to show him the fort, Sherry stayed behind with Mrs. Hill.

She could that Mrs. Hill was distraught and couldn't understand what was going on.

"Mrs. Hill, we believe Jane had been hiding in a fort back behind your house. David and I found it while we were walking earlier. We also believe she has been stealing food and other things from your house after you are asleep."

Mrs. Hill said, "Why would she do that when she knows that she only needs to ask?"

Sherry shook her head and said, "I don't know, but we don't believe she is in her right mind."

Mrs. Hill sighed and said, "Poor baby, I wish she would have just came to me. I would have helped her with whatever she needed."

Sherry reached out and grabbed her hand then said, "I know you would have and if Jane were in her right mind, she would know that also."

Mrs. Hill said, "I hope she is okay. She is so small to be out there all alone."

Sherry replied, "She is a lot stronger than we realize."

David returned a few hours later as Sherry and Mrs. Hill watched several other detectives arrive at the scene and walk towards the fort.

David sat by Sherry on the porch and said, "It doesn't appear she has returned since you and I found the fort."

Sherry nodded and said, "Do you need us to stay with you Mrs. Hill?"

Mrs. Hill nodded and said, "I will be fine, but please let me know if you hear anything, anything at all. I am so worried about Jane."

Sherry nodded and said, "I promise I will." As she leaned in to hug her.

They drove back to the motel, still feeling as if they should have done something else. The detective had promised to call if any news arrived.

David said, "Jane is going to go to Walters, I know she is."

Sherry said, "You mean Tommy is going to go to Walters."

"Whatever you want to call it, but that is where he is going next."

She nodded and said, "Did you tell the detective that we believe that will be the next place she goes?"

He nodded and said, "Yes, and he said that he will go by there once he gets the area swept near the fort."

She nodded and said, "I guess there is nothing else we can do now other than wait."

Tommy had found Walter's small trailer and lurked outside waiting for Walter. He noted Jenny through the window and recognized her right away as the young girlfriend of Walter that insisted on attending the party the night that Stephanie was murdered. She had foolishly left the front door unlocked so he made his way onto the porch.

He knocked and she answered with a smile. She didn't recognize Jane and said, "Well, hello there, can I help you?"

Tommy nodded.

She said, "Who are you?"

With the strength of Tommy, Jane bolted through the door and knocked her down. He ran into the kitchen and grabbed a knife as she cried out, "What the fuck is wrong with you?"

He emerged from the kitchen with a large butcher knife. She ran down the small hallway and hid in a bedroom. He kicked in the door and corned her. He then began stabbing her as she crawled down the hallway slowly.

Sherry took a shower and then laid down on the bed as David was taking his. She heard David's phone ringing while he was in the shower and listened as he answered through the door. She waited for him to come out impatiently to deliver whatever news he had learned. He had a glum look as he came through the door.

She gazed into his eyes and said, "What? Who was that?"

He said, "It was Detective Shultz. He called to tell that he went by Walter's house." He sighed as he looked away. Sweeping his wet hair back he said, "He said, Jenny was stabbed multiple times and lay dead in the living room floor."

Sherry fell back onto the bed, struggling to catch her breath as she fought back tears. She said, "I tried to tell her. Why she wouldn't listen?"

He sat down beside her and held her in his arms as he said, "I know, I know, we tried."

Sherry couldn't sleep and she knew that David wasn't either. They both tossed and turned throughout the night. The next morning, they were not sure what to do. The showered got dressed and then decided to get something to eat. Sherry realized that it was actually a relief for once not to have to worry about Joe searching for her or having to hide every time she went somewhere. Her heart ached at the realization of the price that had been paid for that freedom.

They had breakfast at a small diner near their motel and were eating silently when David's phone rang, it was Detective Schultz. David spoke with him by answering yes and okay several times as Sherry watched intently.

When he hung up, he turned to Sherry and said, "Detective Schultz wants to speak with us today in person."

She nodded and said, "Did he say why?"

He nodded and said, "No, he didn't but he wants to see us in an hour."

She nodded.

They drove to the state police building once they had finished eating and went inside. They waited for Detective Schultz to emerge and gesture for them to follow him.

He directed them both to sit and then said, "I am curious if either one of you know who else might be on Jane's list of victims. We believe she is not going to stop until she is finished with all of them."

David turned to Sherry and said, "I don't know of anyone else, do you?"

Sherry nodded and said, "I believe Walter is high on the list and the only other one that might be would be his sister, Brittney."

Detective Schultz said, "Why do you believe she would be on the list?"

Sherry said, "Because she told me that she was there the night that Stephanie was killed and Tommy would know that she was there."

He nodded and said, "Okay, anyone else?"

Sherry shook her head and said, "No, I don't know of anyone else."

"Are you sure?"

Sherry thought and said, "Brittney told me of all that she knew that was there, but I cannot remember anyone else per say."

He nodded and she said, "Listen, if we could get back in to see Brittney we might could ask her." He grabbed some papers on his desk and began to straighten them and said, "It could take some time to get a court order to visit her. It could be too late by then." He turned to Sherry and said, "I will subpoena a court order and we will go from there." He thanked them and promised to contact if any more news.

They left there and were headed back to their room when Sherry said, "Mark and Joe are both in the hospital aren't they?"

"Yes." David answered

"They both know who was there at that party. We could visit them at the hospital and ask them."

David said, "They are not going to tell us anything."

"They might. It cannot hurt to try."

They drove to the hospital that both men were admitted to and Sherry asked the receptionist to direct her to Joe's room. They were directed to the second floor as Sherry felt her heart beat in her throat on the elevator ride. Once they arrived, they stopped at the reception area where she asked for Joe's room. The receptionist inquired as to who she was and Sherry politely answered that she was his wife.

The nurse hesitantly said, "He is in ICU, this way." They followed her into a room with other patients separated only by curtains. The nurse said, "Ten minutes per visit." As she walked away.

Sherry stood silently staring at him, reflecting on their good times. Absorbing the fact that he was never who she thought he was and wondering how she had been such a fool. The hate was overwhelming and she couldn't help but feel a certain amount of guilt for wanting to beat him herself as he lay there unconscious with nothing but nubs left on his hands. She knew that he would be pissing out of a bag for the rest of his life and never enjoy the touch of a woman again.

She said, "Joe." Then cleared her voice and again said, "Joe, can you hear me? It's me, your wife Sherry."

He nodded his head as he lay there hooked to machines with an oxygen tube through his nose. His eyes slowly opened as he tried to focus. His eyes widened as he noted her standing at the foot of his bed. He began to yell, "You, you fucking bitch!" He tried to raise out of his bed and lunging toward her. He shouted, "I will kill you, you fucking bitch! I will kill you."

The alarms began sounding on his machines as he continued to grab toward her with his bandaged nubs.

The nurse rushed in with a shocked look and demandingly she said, "Go, get out of here, go now." As she tried to pull him back on his bed. Another nurse ran in to administer a sedative through his IV as Sherry and David exited the room.

Once they had left the room and went back into the lobby David said, "I'm sorry, I knew that wouldn't go well but I know you had to try."

Sherry said, "I know it sounds crazy for me to say this, but in a way I feel like it brought a certain amount of closure in seeing him like that. He got what he deserved and Mark did also. The truth is, I am not trying to save Walter either, I am trying to save Jane and unfortunately in order for me to do that, I have to save Walter in the process."

David nodded as he said, "Walter did wrong in hiding and covering the truth but he didn't do intentional harm to people."

Sherry said, "Other than to his own sister."

"You are right, he did cost his sister all of those years of her life."

She suggested that they try to speak with Mark and David reluctantly agreed. They inquired again at reception as to which room he was in. They were directed to the third floor. Sherry didn't know what she was going to say to him, but she felt she needed to look him in the eye as she had done to Joe. They arrived at the third floor and proceeded toward the desk when she noted his wife waiting in the lobby with their two small children. She stopped and watched as the wife appeared tired and worn.

She turned to David and said, "I won't do this to her."

"What?" David asked.

"I can't, I can't do it to her."

He gazed into her eyes and she said, "She doesn't deserve to hear this from me and I cannot lie to her about it either."

She cried, "She was a victim in this, the same as me."

They turned to walk away when Mark's wife called out, "Sherry, Sherry is that you?"

Sherry stopped to see Mark's wife walking toward her. Sherry said, "Oh, I was just here visiting Joe and thought I would see how Mark is doing."

"He is holding his own. I cannot imagine why anyone would want to commit such a heinous crime."

Sherry nodded and said, "I can't either."

"Mark is enjoying visitors right now. Anyone that can show support seems to lift his spirits. Would you like to step in and say hello?"

Sherry said, "Perhaps another day. Right now I need to get back down stairs and check on Joe."

"I thought that was why you came up here? To see Mark."

Sherry said, "I did, really I did. I am just so confused right now and upset. Please forgive me. Of course I would love to step in and say hello to Mark." She smiled as they follow her to a room just a few doors down.

She stopped and said, "I am sorry, I didn't catch your name?" To David.

Sherry chimed in and said, "I am so embarrassed, I should have introduced you. This is my brother, David."

She smiled and said, "It's nice to meet you David."

They entered into the room where Mark lay sleeping with his back turned toward the door.

His wife scrambled to the opposite side of the bed and said, "Mark, guess who I found wondering the halls lost."

He said, "Who?" Lethargically.

"Sherry, Joe's wife."

He quickly turned with a look of fright as his wife stepped back in shock. He realized his outburst and tried to calm himself as he said, "Oh Sherry, how nice of you to stop by."

Sherry nodded her head and said, "How are you feeling?" Tauntingly.

"Never been better" Mark replied as he raised his bandage nubs.

Sherry said, "Well, I hate to hear that happened to you." Sarcastically.

His wife appeared confused as she watched the exchange between them.

Sherry said, "I am sorry, I really should be going now."

She turned to walk out the door as Mark said, "Tell that friend of yours that I said hi and I will see her again someday."

Sherry stopped and turned back to him and said, "I will and you might see her sooner rather than later."

Sherry had taken only one step out the door when the wife said, "Sherry."

She glanced back at her and she said, "I noticed your finger is bandaged as if it were cut off, may I ask what happened?"

Sherry smiled uncomfortably and said, "Oh, this, it was an accident at home in the kitchen." Gesturing toward her finger.

Mark's wife nodded and said, "Wow, what a coincidence." Nodding her head.

Once they had gone down the hall a good distance, Sherry let out a sigh as if she had been holding her breath the entire time they were in visiting with Mark.

David grabbed her arm once they were on the elevator and said, "Are you okay?"

She nodded and said, "Yes, I feel awful for his wife once she learns the truth about her bastard husband."

"Let's pray that she does learn the truth."

Sherry nodded and said, "I feel like their world is crumbling in around them now, much like ours was. The tables have turned David, the tables have turned."

He nodded and said, "I think so too" Half smiling.

The stepped off the elevator and Sherry glanced at her watch noting it to be after three.

She said, "I wonder how Walter took the news of Jenny being murdered."

David nodded his head and said, "He should know by now."

"Let's go back to the detective's office and ask if he has any news."

David nodded and said, "I can call him and ask?" He pulled out his phone and noted he had a missed call from the Detective Schultz. He said, "I guess he tried to call while we were in the hospital. He smiled and said, "He left a voice mail."

He put it on speaker phone and played the message on speaker, "Hello, David when you get this message call me back please." He dialed the number and Aaron answered right away.

He said spoke with him for only minutes when the call ended. Sherry watched intently and said, "What did he say?"

David shook his head and said, "They are giving orders for all officers to consider Jane armed and dangerous. I believe that means if she resist arrest, they are free to take matters into their own hands."

Sherry said, "So, they can shoot her or kill her?"

David nodded.

Tommy had hid behind Walter's trailer and watched from a distance as he had whisked Jenny's body out earlier. He watched Walter set on the steps now and pop open can after can of beer as he hung his head low. Tommy made his way closer to the trailer and entered the bathroom window that he had escaped from after killing Jenny.

He hid in a closet until he heard the door shut and knew that Walter was in for the night. He crept slowly down the hallway and noted Walter sitting on the couch sipping yet another beer. He seen him stack his empty can on his already pyramid of cans on the coffee table. He slowly walked toward the kitchen and opened the refrigerator. He bent down to grab another from the case inside his empty otherwise refrigerator. He sat it on the counter then stopped and stared off with a glum look toward his empty living room.

Tommy struck without warning when he hit Walter in the head with the crescent wrench he had obtained from the tool box in the bedroom. Walter fell to the floor immediately. Tommy moved in quickly as Walter began to moan. Blood pooled from his head as he moaned moving his head back and forth.

Tommy grabbed his pliers as Walter opened his eyes slowly and said, "Why?"

Tommy said, "I loved you and I know what you did."

Walter said, "Who are you?"

Tommy said, "You know who I am."

"Tommy?" Walter said with a confused look.

"That's right, Tommy."

Walter turned his head and cried like a child. Tommy stopped and looked at him confused as he cried, "I am sorry, Tommy. I am so sorry. I deserve whatever you do to me."

"Shut up, shut up Walter" Tommy was angry and quickly grabbed the pliers from his small pink purse and snipped off two of Walters fingers one at a time.

Walter cried out in pain and said, "Tommy, just kill me. I deserve it." Tommy stopped and stepped back and began pacing the room back and forth.

Walter laid in the floor rolling back and forth crying out, "Kill me please, Tommy."

David said, "Sherry, listen to me. We will find her before they do, we have to."

Sherry said, "Where would she go?"

"Let's go back to Walter's trailer." They drove back to Walter's house and noted the lights were off but Walters's car was there. They pulled into the driveway and honked. They couldn't see any movement and it appeared as if no one was there.

David said, "Maybe someone came and picked him up. He probably didn't want to stay here after his wife was murdered in the living room today."

Sherry nodded and said, "Yes, you are probably right." They started to back out of the drive way when Sherry noted a flicker of the curtain in the living room. She said, "David, wait, there is someone in there."

He hit the break and pulled forward again.

Sherry got out and yelled, "Tommy, I know you are in there."

The door opened and Walter opened the door and said, "Tommy isn't here." Sherry noted he looked pale and scared then seen the blood from his left hand drip onto the porch.

She looked back up toward his face and said, "Will you walk down here for a minute so I can talk to you" As she turned to David who was stepping out of the car.

Walter said, "I can't right now, I am busy."

She walked toward him and slowly took the steps up onto the porch. He used his right hand to steady himself on the porch as he appeared lethargic and weak. David followed her up the steps.

Sherry said, "Tommy, come out here right now I want to talk to you."

David grabbed Walter's hand and began slowly assisting him down the steps. He reached for his phone to call the police once he had Walter in the car.

Sherry began to back down the steps behind them. Tommy suddenly stepped out on the steps holding a butcher knife.

Tommy said, "Why did you come here? I wasn't finished."

Sherry said, "Yes Tommy, you are finished."

He wiped his tears as he said, "I wanted them to pay for what they did."

Sherry said, "Tommy, Jane is going to pay for everything that you have done. Do you understand that?"

He sat down on the steps and cried with his head on his knees. Sherry stepped toward him and took the knife from his hands.

She sat down beside him and said, "Tommy, why couldn't you let us handle it?"

He said, "I couldn't. I went crazy. I wanted them to pay."

"I am sorry Tommy, but what you did is wrong. I wanted them to pay also, but not like this."

"They hurt you. They tried to hurt Jane." He wiped his tears and said, "They killed Stephanie and I snapped. I didn't come here to do all of this. I just wanted someone to find out what happened."

Sherry said, "I know Tommy, I know."

"Tommy makes messes. That is what he does, he makes messes." He leaned his head down and cried.

The police arrived as Tommy and Sherry sat on the porch holding each other's hands. Tommy went without provocation into custody as Sherry watched, begging them not to handle his tiny body roughly. Walter was taken away in an ambulance with two of his fingers amputated. The detective told Sherry that Jane would be charged with murder and assault. He said that they should go home and try to rest.

Once Jane was in custody and gone, Sherry and David stood back and watched as they whisked her away at sundown.

David said, "You know that no one is going to believe that Tommy committed those crimes. Jane is going to be held accountable."

Sherry said, "I know, but there has to be something that we can do."

"I will do all that I can, but this is going to be one tough case. The best that we can hope for is that she can get off for temporary insanity and even then she will be sent to a mental institution and still probably never see the light of day."

Sherry cried as David put his arms around her. They went to a motel and Sherry cried herself to sleep.

David said, "We need to get on with our lives. We still don't know what happened to Tommy and we still don't know what happened to my father and I guess we never will. I feel like we need to start to move on."

Sherry said, "But what about Jane?"

"I am going to represent her and do all that I can do. I can't do it from a motel room."

Sherry nodded and said, "Okay."

"Come with me. Come to my home with me and let's work this out together."

She smiled and said, "I don't know, is that what you want?"

"Yes, It is. I want you to come with me."

Sherry and David went to his house in Phoenix and worked on putting their lives together while trying to help Jane with her case. They were allowed to visit once a week and each time it was Jane that they visited. Sherry wondered if Tommy had been able to move on somehow after his revenge was settled. The day of court was scheduled, David had entered a not guilty plea on her behalf. He had subpoenaed Brittney Jones on behalf of Jane.

The prosecutor had Walter, Joe, and Mark all stand against Jane and witness her as the one that had assaulted them. Brittney was asked to step to the witness stand and nervously made her way. David asked her to recount the night that Stephanie was murdered. She told the same story that she had told to Sherry. The jury listened intently. Brittney begged her brother to tell the truth as she cried. Walter seemed to fight back his tears as she pled with him.

The prosecutor argued that Brittney had been declared mentally insane and encouraged the jury to dismiss her statement as if she were a lunatic and had made the entire story up. David asked Jane to come forward and give her own testimonial.

Her tiny, frail body shook as she made her way to the stand. Her delicate voice quivered as she nervously answered time and time again that she couldn't remember any of the events she had been accused of. She was in chains and her tiny body struggled to drag them along as she was escorted to and from the jury stand.

She would glance toward Sherry with pleading eyes as Mark and Joe gave their own testimonials. They both claimed that they had never seen Jane before the day that she attacked them. At the end of the trial, the jury was dismissed and everyone was told that they would be notified once they had made their decision.

Three days later, everyone was called back in to hear the verdict. The jury walked back on one by one as the lined up in their seats. Suddenly, the prosecutor walked forward and began to whisper into the Judge's ear. David turned to look at Sherry confused.

The judge said, "It seems that we have new information that Mr. Jones would like to share.

Walter Jones walked forward to take the stand once more. He was sworn in and seated himself nervously in the box.

The prosecutor said, "Walter, what is that you would like to share with the jury?"

Walter cleared his voice and said, "That girl didn't do this to me." As he pointed to Jane. He said, "That girl didn't do this to any of us." As he turned toward Mark and Joe, he continued, "It was Tommy, Tommy Hill."

The jury looked confused as he said, "Let me explain." He began his story, "My sister told the truth, those two are monsters." He pointed toward Mark and Joe and said, "They got what they deserved and I suppose I did as well. Tommy was my friend and I allowed him to be murdered and his brother to go to prison for a murder he never committed."

Joe stood up and yelled, "You pussy mother fucker, I will kill you."

The judge said, "Shut up and sit down."

Walter continued as he wiped his tears, "My sister told the truth, but what she didn't tell is what she doesn't know. I went to Mark and Joe after she told me that Tommy had seen me place Stephanie's body in Jake Hill's trunk that night. They panicked and told me that we needed to get rid of Tommy. I was scared and didn't know what to do. They told me that if we didn't get rid of Tommy then they would kill everyone in my family and Mrs. Hill also." He cried, "I didn't want to do it but I was scared."

The jury listened intently to his story. Mark stood up and yelled, "Walter, shut the fuck up." As he squirmed in his seat angrily in a panic.

Walter glared at Mark and said, "I don't care Mark. Not anymore anyway. I cannot live with this any longer."

Walter continued, "I went to Tommy and told him that I wanted him to go with me on a drive to see Jake. I knew he would go if it meant seeing his brother. He was like a child and all smiles as we hit the highway. He turned the music up and we headed down the highway toward Tucson. My guilt was overwhelming as I thought about how I would gain the strength to take his life." He stopped to collect his thoughts rubbing his face then said, "I turned off on an old dirt road that Joe had instructed me to. Tommy asked where we were going. I told Tommy that I had to do something that I hoped he would forgive me for. Tommy didn't know what I was talking about.

I felt like I was smothering as I sat there watching for Joe and Mark to show up. Tommy had stepped out of the truck and was collecting rocks when they pulled up. They jumped out and grabbed Tommy and placed a bag over his head. They drug him to their truck and stuck him in the front seat between them. They told me to follow them further down the road. I was so scared I did as they told. We arrived at a small cabin and they drug Tommy in and shoved him into a small dark bedroom and began opening beers and laughing. Playing music. I still remember Tommy's cries from that room.

For three days, we starved him and they would go in and taunt and beat him. I wanted to leave but each time they would tell me that I wasn't leaving with my hands clean. I felt they would kill me also. The night of the third day, they brought him out and told him he had one chance. They told him they were going to fire a shot into the air and he needed to run. They were going to give him an hour head start to make it." He cried as he continued, "They hunted him like a wild animal that night. They had a friend name Fred that stayed at the cabin with me. Within only a few hours, they came dragging his dead body back and told me to bury it." He turned away and said lowly, "He still had his matchbox car in his hand when I pushed him off into his shallow grave. All of this was Tommy's revenge."

The prosecutor asked, "Can you take us to the grave?"

"I spent three days there and it is etched into my mind. I am fairly certain that I can go back."

The prosecutor said, "Is there anything else you can tell us?"

Walter said, "Yes, I held Tommy's hand and pried the matchbox car free. I took it and have it to this day. I carry it with me everywhere I go as a constant reminder of what I did." He reached into his pocket and pulled out a small black matchbox car of a 1973 corvette. He held it up as he sobbed and said, "Tommy loved this car. He never went anywhere without it. I don't think that I should carry it anymore."

Mark and Joe now sat with their heads down sobbing, knowing that they had been caught.

Mark stood up and said, "He is right, we did those things and I want my wife to know I am sorry." He turned toward Joe and said, "It's over Joe, it's time to pay the price. We will never work again or have a life."

Joe said, "No, Mark no."

Mark said, "Yes, it's over."

Chapter 8

Joe stood up as tears ran down his face and said, "He is right, it's over for us now." He turned to Walter and said, "All of our lives have been destroyed and we deserve whatever we get."

Walter nodded.

David turned to Mark and Joe and said, "Did you shoot my father?"

Mark nodded his head and said, "I had Fred do it."

David said, "Did your parents know what you were doing?"

Mark said, "No, they had no idea and thought that Tommy and Jake got what they deserved for what they did to Stephanie."

Suddenly, Jane stood up and in Tommy's voice she said, "Walter, why did you do that to me? I loved you?"

The Jury gasped as the room became silent.

Walter turned to Jane and said, "I am a coward and I am sorry Tommy. I have regretted every day what I did to you. I loved you like a brother and it has taunted me since the day I did it." Tears ran down his face as he said, "Please forgive me?"

Tommy said, "I don't hate you Walter. You have finally set me free. Tommy can go now and move to a better place. I hear that Stephanie is going to be there and puppies. They said we can eat what we want to when we want to and I know Stephanie has been waiting for me. Tell Jake that he is my brother and that I love him. Tell my mother not to worry about me and that I am happy."

Walter cried as Tommy stepped out of Jane's small body. He was wearing his baseball cap that exhibited his school logo. He had his suspenders and navy blue shirt on.

His blue work pants sit high on his waist exposing his white socks. Jane's unconscious body fell backwards as he reached in to kiss her tiny cheek. He waved at Sherry across the room as he walked away, disappearing through the door.

The jury watched in awe as he made his departure. David sat down on the bench and placed his head in his hands near his knees. Tears rolled down Sherry's cheeks as she smiled to wave back. The bailiff came to take Mark, Joe and Walter into custody. They marched out of the room in handcuffs absorbing the new absolution of their fate.

David walked to Sherry with his head down then slowly raised his face to hers and gazed into her eyes. "It's over, it's finally over."

She nodded with a smile and said, "I know, I know." They hugged.

The judge had taken Mark, Joe, and Walter into custody and marched them out of the room. The jury recommended a delay in the sentencing of Jane. She was still going to be held in custody and her fate still rested in the hands of the jury.

Sherry was distraught. "David, why are they still holding her?"

"Because she still killed and assaulted all of those people regardless of what Mark, Joe and Walter did all of those years ago. That will be a completely different trial."

Sherry and David went to Mrs. Hill's house that night. They wanted to be the first ones to deliver the news of what had really happened to Tommy and Jake. Sherry got out of the car to find Mrs. Hill alone on the porch as always. They made their way to her porch as she smiled and waved at their approach. They sat her down and recounted the day's events. Mrs. Hill cried as Sherry told her that Walter had been the one that killed Tommy. She wiped her tears as David explained that Jake would be released and brought home. Sherry tried to explain to her that Tommy had taken over Jane's body and Mrs. Hill seemed to believe her. She prayed for Jane and begged for mercy on her when she goes back to court.

Sherry was anxious and David wanted to request a new hearing. He wanted everyone to have an opportunity to speak on Jane's behalf. Six more months would go by before the court date would come again.

Sherry and David went to visit Jake and deliver the news. They waited for him to be brought in anxiously. He noted it was them from a distance before he picked up the small receiver.

He said, "What have you found out?"

Sherry said, "It is over and they know that you didn't kill Stephanie, I suspect you will be released soon."

"Who did it?"

She said, "My husband and his friends."

He nodded his head and said, "It figures." Then he said, "I don't know what to say. Thank you."

Sherry said, "You are going to be given another chance, I hope you make good of it."

"I used to dream about a day like this, but that was so many years ago." He turned to wipe his tears.

"I could only imagine spending 20 years locked away for a murder that you didn't commit."

He nodded and said, "It is like most of my life was spent here. I don't know where to go or what to do."

"Go home Jake, go home and tell your mother that you love her." He nodded and said, "Does she know?"

206

Sherry nodded and said, "We told her and she is excited. She misses you and she always knew that you didn't kill Stephanie."

He looked into her eyes and said, "I owe you my life."

Sherry nodded and said, "No, you owe your brother your life and I hope you prove to him that you were worth it."

He put his head down and sobbed.

Sherry went back to Mrs. Hill's house once Jake had been set free. She wanted to speak with Jake. He was on the porch with his mother when she arrived. He smiled as she approached. Mrs. Hill quickly jumped up to get Sherry a glass of tea. Sherry asked Jake if he would mind taking a small walk with her. He agreed.

They began walking toward the old fort in the back yard and she said, "Jake do you ever wonder what happened to the baby that you had with Lynn?"

He said, "I have thought about it off and on over the years. I assume she terminated the pregnancy, why?"

Sherry said, "She didn't terminate the pregnancy and I think I know where the child is."

"What, what are you talking about?"

Sherry said, "I believe that Jane may be your daughter. I think that is why Tommy chose her. I think he knew who she was."

Jake's eyes widened as he stepped back and leaned over to catch his breath. He said, "Really?"

Sherry nodded and said, "There is only one way to find out."

"Are you suggesting a DNA test?"

"Yes, but I don't want to tell your mother yet, not until we know for sure. I mean she loves Jane to death regardless, but I think it is best we keep it a secret until we are certain."

He said, "I would love to take the test."

She smiled and said, "I am going to visit Jane on Friday. I will ask her if she is willing to take the test with you."

He smiled and said, "My brother is still speaking to me from above. I wish he was here to share in the joy that has been brought to me." He reached out and hugged her and said, "I owe you so much and I can never repay you."

"You owe me nothing other than a promise to be good and take care of your mother."

"That I can do."

Sherry went to visit Jane that Friday afternoon. Jane appeared frail and thin as she walked toward the glass window to speak through the receiver.

Sherry said, "Jane, are you okay?"

Jane said, "How much longer am I going to have to be kept like this?"

"I have no idea, but David and I are both working nonstop to get you out."

Jane nodded and said, "I don't understand why I can't just go home. Is it because you don't want me anymore?"

Sherry said, "No, Jane that is not it." Sherry turned away and said, "Listen to me Jane, you have got to be strong and pull through this. You are going to be released soon."

"I don't like it here and I don't have any friends here."

"Jane, I want to share some information with you but I am not sure how to tell you."

Jane looked at her intently and said, "What is it?"

Sherry sighed and said, "I believe that I may have found your real family but I am not totally sure. It would require a DNA test."

Jane stepped back from the glass window and said, "I knew it, you don't want to be my family anymore." Tears ran down her cheeks as she threw the receiver and ran.

Sherry stood up and cried out, "Wait, Jane wait, let me explain."

Sherry lowered her head and turned to walk away. She cried on her way home and wished she hadn't mentioned the DNA test to Jane. She waited for David to come home and told him what had happened.

He said, "I have an idea. Let me see if we can collect some DNA from her without her knowing. I have many connections at the jail."

Sherry smiled and said, "That would be wonderful. I will go get a collection from Jake today."

Sherry drove out and spoke with Jake and explained to him that she needed to collect his specimen. He quickly swabbed his mouth and provided it. She stayed for several hours and visited with Mrs. Hill. Jake was in good spirits as was Mrs. Hill.

Jake sat down and said, "I have wonderful news to tell you."

Sherry asked, "What is it?"

"They seem to have an opening for a mechanic where Walter used to work and have agreed to give me a shot."

Sherry smiled and said, "That is wonderful Jake, I hope you like it."

"I know that this is going to be an adjustment for me. I didn't realize how much everything changes over 20 years but I am determined to make it."

She smiled and said, "Just take it slow and you will be fine."

Mrs. Hill said, "I want to know what is going on with Jane? Have you heard anything?"

Sherry said, "The court date has been rescheduled for next month. I think she would love it if the two of you were able to attend and show support."

Mrs. Hill smiled and said, "I would love to, Jake?" As she turned toward him.

He nodded and said, "I wouldn't miss it. We will be there."

Sherry left there and drove home with the specimen in hand. Mrs. Hill had no idea that Jane could be her granddaughter and she smiled at the thought. She arrived home and David was already there.

She threw the specimen on the table and said, "I got it, the specimen, I got it."

He nodded his head and said, "I went to the jail today to see about getting the specimen."

Sherry said, "Alright" Noticing the concerned look on his face.

He said, "Sit down." Pointing to the couch.

She felt her heart begin the race and knew that he had bad news. She said, "What is it?" As she sat down.

"It's Jane, she tried to kill herself today."

Sherry jumped up and said, "What? Is she okay?"

David nodded and said, "Yes, they found her in time. She had somehow managed to slice her wrist, but they got her in time. She was taken to the County General Hospital."

Sherry said, "We need to go see her." He nodded as he grabbed the car keys and walked toward the door.

The arrived to find her lying awake looking out the window. Her wrist were bandaged and she appeared tiny, frail. Listless, and lonely.

Sherry ran to her and said, "Jane, why?"

Jane turned her head away from Sherry and said, "You don't love me anymore, I know you don't."

Sherry said, "Jane that is not true."

Jane said, "Apparently, I have killed several people and hurt others. I don't even remember doing it and I might do it again." She cried and said, "I could even hurt you." As she wiped her tears.

Sherry said, "Jane, you didn't hurt anyone. That wasn't you, it was Tommy."

Jane said, "Then how come I can't go home?"

Sherry said, "You're going to go home, but first we have to prove that you didn't do those things." Sherry leaned her head down and cried as she held Janes hand. She said, "Jane, I want you to come home more than I want anything. I thought I was helping you when I suggested that your family might be the Hills."

Jane's eyes lit up and she said, "Mrs. Hill?"

Sherry nodded and said, "Yes, I was going to tell you but you ran away to quick."

Jane scooted up higher in her bed and said, "What are you talking about?"

"I don't want to give you false hope, but I found out that Jake had a child 20 years ago that was given up for adoption. Jane, it could be you. That child could be you."

Jane said, "Really?" Smiling.

Sherry nodded her head and said, "I don't know for sure and I don't want to end up disappointing you either. It is important that you understand that Mrs. Hill doesn't know and she loves you anyway."

Jane smiled and said, "I love her too."

"Can we do a DNA test and find out?" Sherry asked.

Jane nodded and said, "I am scared that we are wrong though and then I will not be her granddaughter."

"Jane, Mrs. Hill cannot love you anymore than she already does anyway."

"I know, and I cannot love her any more than I do already either."

"Can we do this test for Jake?"

Jane smiled and said, "Yes, we can do the test for Jake."

David pulled a small box from his pocket and said, "We already have Jakes specimen and now all that we need is yours." Pointing to the box.

Jane smiled and said, "What are we waiting for?"

He quickly opened the package and revealed the swab. She opened her mouth as he gathered the specimen. He sealed it and sat it on the table.

He turned to Sherry and said, "Do you have Jake's?"

She nodded and said, "I do." She grabbed her purse and pulled it out, handing it to David.

Once David had left the room in route to the lab, Jane said, "How long will it be before we know the results?"

Sherry said, "I don't know. I assume David will ask."

Jane said, "Do you think Jake will be happy or sad if I am his daughter?"

"He is excited and wants you to be his daughter. He and Mrs. Hill have already made plans to attend your next hearing."

Jane nodded and said, "That's good. I want Mrs. Hill to be there. I will feel better if she is there."

Sherry smiled and said, "I know you will." She reached out and hugged Jane and said, "Jane I don't want you to ever think that I don't love you anymore. You are like my little sister and I couldn't imagine life without you."

Jane smiled and said, "I am glad we had this talk."

Sherry laughed.

David returned 30 minutes later and said, "The results will be in by morning."

Sherry said, "That is wonderful." She turned to Jane and said, "We will be back early in the morning for the results to be read."

Jane smiled and said, "I probably will not be able to sleep all night."

Sherry and David went home and nervously waited for the morning. David suggested that they call Jake in for the reading of the results, but Sherry didn't think that they should do that in case she was wrong and Jane wasn't who she thought she was. They drove to the hospital and awaited the results. Sherry and Jane played cards while David paced the floor and left to go check the lab every thirty minutes.

It was noon before he came back with an envelope in hand. He was smiling eagerly and said, "Who wants to do the honors?"

Sherry stepped toward him and he handed her the envelope as he gazed into her eyes. She turned toward Jane and said, "Jane, before I read this I want you to promise me that this will change nothing if the results come back that you are not Jake's daughter."

Jane said, "I thought we had this talk last night?"

Sherry smiled and said, "We did, but still I am afraid that this will change things and I don't want it to change anything."

"It isn't going to change my love for Mrs. Hill. I have a family already and that will not prove anything to me."

Sherry smiled and sat beside her and hugged her. Sherry said, "I am your family and so is David. Don't ever forget that. Mrs. Hill is your grandmother regardless what this sill paper says."

Jane nodded and said, "That is right." Smiling.

The guards that stood outside her room were listening in and Sherry could sense they were also excited to hear the verdict. Jane had a magnetic personality and everyone that met her loved her. Her innocence consumed everyone she touched. Sherry slowly tore the envelope open and removed the small folded paper that was packed inside. She unfolded it and then gazed back toward Jane. Her expression was serious and intent. Jane felt as if it were not the news she had expected.

David said, "It doesn't change anything Jane." Assuming from her expression that they were wrong.

Sherry said, "Jane," Then sighed and said, "Jane Smith, how would you feel about becoming Jane Hill?"

The guards began to smile and laugh and David laughed as he hugged Sherry. Jane's mouth dropped and her expression was priceless. She couldn't close her mouth and brought her hands up to cover it. She was elated and Sherry had never seen her more happy.

Once Jane was able to gain her composure she kept repeating, "Really, are you sure?"

Sherry said, "Its right here, do you want to see it?" Handing Jane the paper. Jane looked away then Sherry realized that she had forgotten that Jane cannot read. She said, "I'm sorry, but yes really. You are legally and officially a Hill."

Jane was all smiles for the remainder of the day. She wanted to call Mrs. Hill right away and tell her but Sherry wanted to surprise her. Sherry suggested that they have a small party in the room. The guards agreed to let Mrs. Hill and Jake into the room that afternoon. David and Sherry ran out and bought a cake and punch to celebrate. Sherry called Jake and told him that they were going to announce the results that afternoon and suggest that he and Mrs. Hill come to the hospital at two. They arrived and Jake noted the cake and punch right away.

Sherry said, "Mrs. Hill I assume you are wondering why you are here?"

Mrs. Hill said, "Jake told me that Jane was in the hospital and we were going to visit." She turned to Jane and said, "Are you alright dear?" She leaned in to hug her. She glanced around the room and said, "Is it your birthday Jane?"

Jane smiled and said, "Yes, yes it is my birthday."

Sherry asked Mrs. Hill to sit down next to Jake in the chair. She opened the results and read them. Jake jumped up and hugged Jane and then his mother. Sherry stood up to explain to Mrs. Hill what had happened.

Mrs. Hill teared up and said, "Oh my dear, I always knew that there was something special about you, but I didn't need a piece of paper to tell me that I loved you."

Jane smiled and said, "I said the same thing."

Mrs. Hill said, "From now on though, you will be calling me grandma."

Jane laughed and said, "Okay, grandma."

Jake said, "I know that you really don't know me, but I aim to be a good man and father. We have lots of time to get to know each other."

Jane nodded and said, "I know I can tell you are a good person."

He smiled and said, "I am aiming to be."

They ate cake and drank punch together that afternoon. Sherry felt as if things were going to turn out okay for Jane but she couldn't help but worry about the impending trial.

Jane returned to jail the following weekend. It made it much more difficult to visit her then when she was in the hospital but Sherry knew that Jane was in higher spirits and that made it a little easier.

The court room was full of people that had taken an interest in the case as Sherry made her way into the room. She sat close to the front so that she could be close to David. He was representing Jane in the case. David called Brittney in again as a witness first and she once again recounted the night of Stephanie's murder. He called Jane in as a witness and had told her to tell the truth. She walked slowly with her chains dragging to the stand and David sensed her nervousness. He asked her to introduce herself.

She said, "I am Jane Hill."

The judge turned to David in a confused manor.

David said, "She recently found out her true identity."

The judge nodded and said, "Continue."

David said, "What do you remember about the nights that Mark, Joe, Jenny and Walter were assaulted or killed?"

She nodded and said, "Nothing, I don't remember nothing."

David said, "It's going to be okay Jane." She was sobbing. He said, "Jane, had you ever met Jenny, Walter or Mark before?"

She nodded and said, "No, I don't know who they are."

He said, "Jane, what do you think happened?"

She said, "It was Tommy, he was living inside my head. He would sometimes take over my mind and it wouldn't be me anymore. He told me that Mark and Joe killed Stephanie and then they started hunting kids with handicaps and killing them for years after that. He said that he had to stop them before they did it to someone else."

David nodded and said, "Thank you Jane."

Next, David called the therapist up to give report of her mental evaluation of Jane. She was sworn in and sat down. She introduced herself as Dr. Leanne Johnson. David approached her and said, "Dr. Johnson have you met with Jane Hill?"

She nodded and said, "Yes, I met with her on several occasions." She smiled and said, "She is a fascinating girl."

David said, "In your professional opinion, do you believe she is mentally competent?"

She nodded and said, "No, not at all. She is delusional and believes that someone named Tommy has possessed her." Sherry turned to see Mrs. Hill and Jake near the back of the room watching.

David said, "Do you believe she is telling the truth?"

She smiled and said, "I believe that she believes she is telling the truth."

He said, "Thank you." He gave the prosecutor the opportunity to question her. The prosecutor was a younger man that wore shoes that clicked with each step on the hard tile floor. He wore and expensive suit and tie and appeared he would never allow a hair to be out of place.

He approached her and said, "Mrs. Johnson, in her professional opinion do you believe that Jane is a danger to society?"

She replied, "I believe that something caused her to snap. I believe that she remembered her captors and wanted revenge on Mark and Joe and she set out to have it. I have yet to understand why she attacked Walter and Jenny."

He said, "That is all." Waving his hand to dismiss the witness.

David called Walter to the stand as a hostile witness. He was sworn in and seated himself in the box.

David said, "Walter do you believe this girl?" Pointing to Jane, "Is the girl that attacked you that night?"

Walter shook his head and said, "I believe it was Tommy in that girl's body. She sounded exactly like Tommy and she acted like Tommy but she looked like her."

She prosecutor stood up and said, "Enough with this nonsense, it was either her or it wasn't."

Walter said, "Then it wasn't." The prosecutor sat down shaking his head, angrily.

David brought Mark in as a hostile witness. Mark took the stand as Sherry watched his nubby fingers fidgeting. David approached him and asked him to introduce himself to the court. He was chained and wore a blue jumpsuit issued by the jail.

Mark introduced himself and David said, "Do you believe that this girl assaulted you the night you were attacked?"

Mark shook his head and said, "I know it was Tommy Hill that assaulted me. He looked like her but he talked like Tommy. That tiny girl had the strength of Tommy Hill. He recounted things that only Tommy could recount."

David said, "How many handicapped kids did you and Joe kill during the 20 years that you spent hunting and trapping them?"

Mark looked down at his nubby fingers and said, "At least 30, if not more."

David said, "Was Tommy killed during one of your hunting expeditions?"

"Yes."

"Was this girl a victim to one of your hunting expeditions?"

"Yes."

"Do you have anything that you would like to share with the court?"

"I do, I want the court to know that this girl is not a murderer, she is a victim. I don't believe that she is the one that attacked me." He sighed and said, "Even if she had been the one that attacked me, I deserved it. My life is over and I am trying to come to terms with that. I don't believe that hers should be over as well." He looked out into the courtroom at his wife that sit watching as he testified with tears in her eyes.

David dismissed the witness and the prosecutor made his approach.

The prosecutor said, "So, the person that attacked you looked like her?" Pointing to Jane.

Mark nodded and said, "Yes."

"But you don't think it was her?"

"No, I don't." Mark shook his head.

"So, you think it was a man that you killed 20 years ago that attacked you?"

Mark said, "Yes,"

The prosecutor said, "Dismissed" As he waved his hand and walked away.

David said, "I would like permission to approach the witness again."

The judge said, "Agreed."

David walked toward Mark and said, "I want you to think about this before you give your answer."

Mark said, "Okay."

"Can you positively identify Jane as the person that attacked you?" Pointing to Jane.

Mark sat quietly for a moment and then said, "No, I cannot."

David said, "That is all your honor."

He requested permission to bring Walter back to the stand. Walter was sworn back in and sat in the witness stand uneasy. David said, "I want you to think long and hard before you answer this question."

Walter said, "Okay."

David said, "Can you positively without a doubt identify this woman as the one that attacked you?" Pointing to Jane.

Walter looked at Jane and then looked down as he shook his head and said, "No, I cannot."

David approached the stand asked for permission to bring Joe in. Joe was brought in wearing shackles and the same blue jumpsuit that Walter and Mark wore. He looked thin and weak as Sherry watched intensely as he took the stand and was sworn in. He appeared weak and broken and not the arrogant self- absorbed prick she remembered.

David asked him, "Who attacked you the night that you were attacked?"

He said, "It was her." Pointing to Jane.

"How do you know it was her? Did you see her?"

"I don't know." Joe lowered his head.

David said, "In your testimony you said that you were struck with spray in your face and then knocked unconscious so, how do you know it was her?"

"I don't know."

"Well, you are sitting here pointing a finger at her and so I would assume that somehow you seen her and know it was her. Did you ever once see her?"

He put his head down and nodded and said, "No, I suppose that I never did see her."

"So it is safe to say that you are not really sure who attacked you?"

Joe didn't answer.

David said, "Answer the court Joe, Is it safe to say that you are not really sure who attacked you?"

Joe said, "Yes." Very lightly.

David said, "Speak up the court cannot hear you."

"Yes, it is safe to say."

David waved his hand and said, "Dismissed." The prosecutor was giving opportunity to readdress the witness and declined. The closing arguments began.

The prosecutor went first. He stood up and tapped his shoes across the floor to approach the jury. He placed his index finger over his lips as he perched them appearing to be in deep thought.

He said, "I realize to most of you sitting here today that she appears to be a tiny, innocent, frail, little girl. But, in reality she is a monastery, and evil monster that has created many terrible crimes against our people. She brutally attacked and killed a woman named Brittney Jones, a woman she didn't even know that had done absolutely nothing to her and that didn't even know her." He turned toward the court room and said, "She is evil, and deserves to pay for her crime. She brutally attacked this man." Pointing to Joe, he continued, "Yes, he may have committed his own crimes, but it wasn't her job to have him answer for them it was the courts. She has tried to take the law into her own hands and we cannot allow that.

His life has changed forever. For Christ sake, he cannot even eat or do simple things anymore as a person. She stripped him of his manhood and left him for dead. She is monster and we cannot allow her to walk free." He turned to Mark and said, "What about this man? She stripped him of his life as well and she had never even met him either." He tapped his shoes back toward the jury and leaned onto their bench forward to face them and said, "She is a woman without mercy, these men she attacked have not been convicted of a crime and she tried to take to law into her own hands. She tried to rob us of our right to a trial by jury as Americans. It is our job as Americans to not lose our rights to people like her. She should be convicted and be made to answer for her crimes. Please, I beg you not to let her innocence fool you. It is up to each of you today to do the right thing and make her answer for her crimes."

He waved his hand as he walked away and said, "That is all."

David stood up and cleared his voice as he proceeded toward the jury. He stood in front of them and said, "Each of you have heard the testimony here today." He turned toward Walter and said, "You heard Walter, he said that she didn't attack him. He said it was in fact Tommy Hill that attacked him, not her. Then you heard Mark testify. He said that she didn't attack him, in his own words he said that it was in fact Tommy Hill that attacked him. These two men do not know who attacked them and both testified that a man that they killed attacked them. Then we heard Joe come up and say it was her, but when he was questioned he admitted that he doesn't know for sure either because whoever did attack him, he never seen them.

We heard Jane testify on her own behalf and she said that she has no recollection of attacking any of them." He turned to Jane and said, "It is our responsibility as Americans to do the right thing. We cannot convict unless we believe someone committed the crime without a reasonable doubt."

He smiled and said, "If that is not a reasonable doubt then I don't know what is. She doesn't remember doing it and the victims themselves saying that she didn't do it. Please, I beg of you, do not convict someone that her own attackers cannot testify that they know it was her that did it. We have a responsibility to society to do the right thing as Americans and to convict someone simply on hearsay is not American." He waved his hand as he walked away and said, "That is all."

The prosecutor stood back up and walked slowly toward the jury again. He leaned his head down and said, "If we allow this woman to walk free then we allow everything that our justice system stands for to be an injustice. This woman is a monster and if we set her free then we allow her to do what she has done to these men to happen to others. You have a responsibility to this country to take someone like this off the streets. If you fail today then you fail this country."

He waved his hand and said, "That is all." As he walked back to his seat.

Court was dismissed and everyone was informed that they would be notified when the jury makes it decision. Sherry and David went to eat with Mrs. Hill and Jake when they left.

Jake said, "I was really impressed with the direction that you took the case."

David said, "I am just hoping that the jury buys it."

Jake said, "I wish I had you as my lawyer when I got convicted." Smiling.

David said, "Let's not get too excited. The verdict isn't in yet."

Sherry said, "Well, no matter I want to thank you and tell you that I am proud of how you handled it also."

David smiled and said, "Let's just hope it works."

Mrs. Hill said, "How long do you think it will take for the jury to make a decision?"

David said, "Sometimes it is hours or minutes and other times it can be days."

Sherry was so anxious that she couldn't sit still. They went home and she constantly paced the floor.

David said, "Please, you may as well sit down and relax it could be a while before they reach a verdict."

Sherry said, "I keep going over and over in my head how we will explain to her that she is possibly going to prison if they find her guilty."

He said, "If they find her guilty then I will move for a motion to have her declared mentally insane." he sighed and said, "If we do have to declare her mentally insane she will probably never be free again, you do understand that don't you?"

Sherry nodded and said, "I don't want to think about that right now. What about Brittney? She has spent most of her life in a mental hospital locked up and she should be set free as well."

David said, "I know. I have been thinking about that. I am going to file an appeal to have her re-evaluated after we get through this. It isn't fair that she was locked up for knowing the truth and someone needs to stand up for her."

Sherry stood up and walked toward him with a smile and said, "That is why I love you so much. You always know the right thing to say."

His phone rang and he smiled as he looked at the number. He answered then hung up and said, "They have reached a verdict."

Sherry was so nervous on the drive over that David had to pull over once so that she could throw up.

He called Jake while she was vomiting and said, "The verdict is in."

Jake said, "We are on our way."

They arrived and David approached seated himself waiting on Jane to be brought in to sit next to him. Sherry sat one row back. Jake and Mrs. Hill arrived just moments later and sat with Sherry. They brought Jane in and seated her next to David. She appeared nervous and fidgeted in her seat and they brought the jury in. They filed in one at a time taking their seats.

The judge struck his gavel on the desk several times and cited, "Here, here all in session. Has the jury reached a verdict?"

The juror at the far end stood up and said, "Yes, judge we have."

He said, "Please read the verdict."

The juror slowly opened the envelope and began, "We the jury find the defendant not guilty on the charge of murder."

The court room became loud and anxious as the judge struck his gavel again and said, "Continue with the verdict."

The juror continued, "We the jury find the defendant not guilty on the charge of assault with intent to kill."

David stood up and smiled at Sherry as Jane hugged him. Sherry stood up with tears in her eyes and she ran forward to hug Jane.

The judge said, "The defendant will be released at once."

Jane was wiping her tears as Mrs. Hill sat crying with Jake hugging her. Jane was released that afternoon, released of all charges and released to live a normal life. She didn't know what a normal life was since she had never had one but she felt as if she had something to look forward to. They went to Mrs. Hill's house to celebrate afterwards.

The night grew late and Sherry asked Jane, "Jane, are you ready to go home?"

Jane turned to her and said, "Sherry, I am home."

Sherry smiled and said, "I kind of thought that you might say that."

Jane went to her and said, "I owe everything to you. I don't want you to be upset but I feel like this is home."

"I am not upset with you. I am glad that you found your home."

Mrs. Hill wiped her tears and said, "I think that you should take Tommy's old room. He would have wanted that."

The doorbell rang and Mrs. Hill sent Jake to get it. They were all in the kitchen gathered around the table when he brought Brittney in.

Brittney said, "I am sorry, I didn't want to interrupt your party."

Sherry stood up and turned to her and said, "No, we are glad to you see you."

Brittney said, "The judge ordered that I be released once the proper paperwork had been filed. I have been out for several weeks. I was at the court room today when Jane was found not guilty."

Sherry said, "We had talked about helping you next but it looks like it already worked out."

Brittney smiled and said, "I went to see Walter and thanked him for finally doing the right thing. I needed to forgive him in order to move on with my life."

David said, "I hope that you can put this all behind you now."

She said, "It will not be easy but I intend to enjoy what I have left."

Jake said, "Please, sit down." He offered her tea and she accepted.

Mrs. Hill said, "You are welcome here anytime, I want you to know that."

She said, "Thank you, this means a lot since I have no one left now."

Sherry said, "Where are you staying?"

She said, "Right now I am at Walter's old trailer. He owned it and told me to take it. He gave me his truck also, at least I can get around and find a job."

Jake said, "I will try to help you anyway that I can."

David said, "I might be able to as well."

Brittney said, "I appreciate that, I really do. But, the reason I came here today is because Walter released everything to me and I wanted to give you this." She pulled out the Matchbox car that belonged to Tommy.

Mrs. Hill said, "Tommy's corvette, he loved that car."

She handed it to Mrs. Hill and said, "I wanted you to have it because I know that is what Tommy would have wanted."

Mrs. Hill began crying as she held the small car in her hand. She reached out to Jane and said, "I believe that Tommy would have wanted you to have this, not me." Jane looked shocked as she turned to Sherry, Sherry nodded for her to take it.

Brittney said, "I should be leaving now."

Jake said, "Please stay a while unless you have something else to do?"

She smiled and said, "Not really, nothing other than sitting by myself in that old trailer."

"How about we play a round of dominoes? What do you say Jane? I hear you are pretty good." Jake smiled.

Jane smiled and said, "I am pretty good."

Sherry and David gathered their things to head home and Sherry glanced back as she went out the door to the picturesque family gathered around the kitchen table playing dominoes with smiles on their faces. Somehow, it felt more right than anything she had ever known before. She glanced down at her finger that had been cut off that night at the cabin and realized that it wouldn't be constant reminder of that night it would instead be a constant reminder of a small price she paid for this day to come to be.

The end